This
You m

D1179216

A Duke
in Danger

A Duke
in Danger

Barbara Cartland

G.K. Hall & Co. • Chivers Press
Waterville, Maine USA   Bath, England

This Large Print edition is published by G.K. Hall & Co., USA and by Chivers Press, England.

Published in 2002 in the U.S. by arrangement with International Book Marketing Limited.

Published in 2002 in the U.K. by arrangement with Cartland Promotions.

U.S. Softcover 0-7862-3962-X (Paperback Series)
U.K. Hardcover 0-7540-4866-7 (Chivers Large Print)
U.K. Softcover 0-7540-4867-5 (Camden Large Print)

The text of this Large Print edition is unabridged.
Other aspects of the book may vary from the original edition.

Set in 16 pt. Plantin by Elena Picard.

Printed in the United States on permanent paper.

British Library Cataloguing-in-Publication Data available

Library of Congress Cataloging-in-Publication Data

Cartland, Barbara, 1902–
    A duke in danger / Barbara Cartland.
      p. cm.
    ISBN 0-7862-3962-X (lg. print : sc : alk. paper)
    1. Napoleonic Wars, 1800–1815 — Veterans — Fiction.
  2. Inheritance and succession — Fiction. 3. Administration of estates — Fiction. 4. Large type books. I. Title.
  PR6005.A765 D85 2002
    823′.912—dc21   2001056364

Author's Note

The Army of Occupation in France after the defeat of Napoleon presented an enormous problem of organisation. The French thought that the feeding of 150,000 troops would be a miracle, and their attitude towards the force swung from welcome to resentment.

What was more, the French were protesting that they would not pay their indemnity, and Madame de Staël predicted it would be paid "in gold the first year, in silver the second, and in the third in lead."

The occupaton finally ended after the Congress of Aix-la-Chapelle in November 1818. But in England there were two different enemies — political agitation and economic destress. The soldiers returning home found that in the country for which they had fought so valiantly, there was no place for heroes.

Chapter One

1818

The Duke of Harlington arrived at Harlington House in Berkeley Square and looked round him with satisfaction.

The house was obviously in excellent repair, and he viewed with pride the portraits of his ancestors on the walls and up the stairs.

There were also the paintings collected by a previous Duke which included a number of those by French Masters.

He had just come from France, where he had learnt to recognise the genius of the French artists in a way he had been unable to do before the war with Napoleon.

However, he was intelligent enough to realise that since the end of the war he had increased his knowledge of a great number of things in which he had not been interested previously.

A tall, extremely handsome man, his years as a soldier had left their mark on the way he walked, and perhaps too in the expression in his eyes.

Women, and there had been a great number of them, had said to him that he always appeared to be looking for something below the surface and generally to be disappointed.

He was not quite certain what they meant, but he had learnt to judge men and women by their fundamental personalities rather than by their superficial qualities.

He had indeed owed his very important position in Wellington's Army to his understanding of human nature.

He was not only a leader, but, as someone had once said of him, he had that extra quality of magnetism which is found only in the greatest Rulers.

It was a compliment that had made the Duke laugh when he heard it. At the same time, because he was not in the least conceited, he hoped it was true.

Now as he walked from the Hall into the downstairs Sitting-Room and from there into the book-filled Library, he thought few men could have been as fortunate in life as he had been.

He had survived five gruelling years in Portugal and Spain, then in France and finally at Waterloo, without receiving a scratch, when so many of his friends and contemporaries had been killed beside him.

Then, because of his outstanding ability not only as a soldier but as a diplomat, he had become essential to the Iron Duke during the Years of Occupation.

Looking back on them, they had undoubtedly been troubled times of frustration and political drama that concerned not only Britain but the whole of Europe.

Yet now, though it seemed incredible, it was over, and by the end of the year — it was now three years after Waterloo — the Army of Occupation would have come home.

After all the dramatic discussions, the tension of rising tempers, the decisions made and unmade, combined with the endless tug-of-war between the Allies, the Duke could hardly believe that he was at this moment, a free man.

There was still the Congress of Aix-la-Chapelle which was to take place in October, but the Army was to be out of France by November 30.

As far as the Duke of Harlington was concerned, he had now his own personal problems to settle, for Wellington had reluctantly allowed him to leave the Army at the beginning of the summer so that he could put his own affairs in order.

It was a pleasant surprise to arrive in London to find that Harlington House at any rate seemed in fairly good shape.

He had sent one of his *Aides-de-Camp*, an extremely trustworthy man, ahead of him, with instructions to see that the staff was notified of his arrival.

He intended to stay under his own roof while

he called on the Prince Regent, and if the King was well enough, to call on His Majesty at Buckingham Palace.

It was strange to be back in England after so many years abroad, but stranger still to know that his position in life was now very different from what it had been when he was last here.

Then as Ivar Harling, one of the youngest Colonels in the British Army, he had found a great deal to amuse him, most of which was unfortunately well beyond his purse.

Now as the Duke of Harlington he was not only a distinguished aristocrat with many hereditary duties which had to be taken up, but also an extremely wealthy man.

Letters which had been waiting for him at Paris from the late Duke's Bankers enclosed not only a list of the possessions which were now his but also a statement of the money which was standing in his name.

The amount of it seemed incredible, but as there was still so much to do for Wellington, the new Duke had set his own needs on one side and put his country first.

When he reached the Library, he stood looking at the leather-bound books which made the walls a patchwork of colour and appreciated the very fine painting of horses by Stubbs over the mantelpiece.

The Butler, an elderly man, came into the room.

He was followed by a footman who was carrying a silver tray on which there was a wine-cooler engraved with the family crest and containing an open bottle of champagne.

When a glass was poured out for the Duke, he noticed automatically that the footman's livery did not fit well and his stockings were wrinkled.

It was with some difficulty that he did not point it out to the man and tell him to smarten himself up.

Then as the footman set down the tray on a table in the corner of the room, the Butler hesitated, and the Duke understood that he had something to say.

"What is it?" he enquired. "I think your name is Bateson."

"Yes, Your Grace. That's right."

There was a pause, then he began again a little hesitatingly:

"I hopes Your Grace'll find everything to your liking, but we've only had three days to prepare for your visit, and the house has been shut up for the last six years."

"I was thinking how well it looked," the Duke replied pleasantly.

"We've worked hard, Your Grace, and while I presumed to engage several women to clean every room that Your Grace was likely to use, there's a great deal more to be done."

"I suppose since the late Duke was so ill in the last years of his life," the Duke said reflectively, "and did not come to London, you were down to a skeleton staff."

"Just my wife and myself, Your Grace."

The Duke raised his eye-brows.

"That certainly seems very few in so large a house. Yet," he added graciously, "it certainly looks as I expected."

"It's what I hoped Your Grace'd say," the Butler replied, "and if I have your permission to enlarge the staff further, I feel certain we can soon get things back to what they were in the old days."

"Of course!"

The Duke twitched his lips at the Butler's words.

Already references to "the old days" had become a joke in the Army, in diplomatic and political circles, and, he was quite certain, in domestic ones too.

Every country, and he had visited a great number since peace had been declared, had talked of nothing but the old days and how good things were then, compared to what they were now.

He was quite sure that it was something that would be repeated to him again and again in England.

Then, as if Bateson realised that he had no wish to go on talking, he said:

"Luncheon'll be ready very shortly, Your Grace. I hopes it'll be to your liking."

The Duke thought that the man was almost pathetically eager to please, and when Bateson shut the door behind him he wondered how old he was.

He remembered that when he was a small boy

and his father had brought him to this house, Bateson had been there, and he had thought him very impressive with six stalwart footmen behind him as he greeted them in the Hall.

"It was a long time ago," the Duke said to himself.

By now Bateson must be well over sixty, but he could understand that having been in Ducal service all his life, the man had no wish either to make a change or to retire earlier than he need.

The Duke was well aware that there was widespread unemployment in England and it would obviously be difficult for an elderly man to get a job.

Besides which, with men released from the Army of Occupation coming home every month, the situation would become more and more difficult.

He remembered the fuss there had been when the Duke of Wellington had proposed a reduction of thirty thousand men in the Army.

Then he told himself that with the wealth he now owned, there was no need for him to make any reductions in staff; in fact, he would increase it in every house he owned.

When he went into the Dining-Room to eat an excellent luncheon served by Bateson with the help of two footmen, he decided that his first task, now that he was back in England, should be to visit his new home, Harlington Castle, in Buckinghamshire.

Even now, after he had thought about it for

two years, he could hardly believe that it was his and that he was, incredibly and unexpectedly, the fifth Duke of Harlington!

He was exceedingly proud to belong to a family that had played its part in the history of England since the time of the Crusades.

However, he had never in his wildest dreams thought that he might succeed to the Dukedom.

He had always been sensible enough to realise that he was a very unimportant member of the Harlings. His father had been only a cousin of the previous Duke, and there had been three lives between him and any chance of inheritance.

But just as the war had brought devastation and misery to so many households over the whole of Europe, the previous Duke's only son, Richard, had been killed at Waterloo.

Ivar Harling had seen Richard just before the battle, and he had been in tremendous spirits.

"If we do not defeat the Froggies once and for all this time," he had said cheerfully, "then I will bet you a dinner at White's to a case of champagne that the war will last another five years."

Ivar Harling had laughed.

"Done, Richard!" he said. "I have the feeling I shall be the loser, but it will be in a good cause!"

"It certainly will!" Richard replied with a grin; then he had added: "Seriously, what is our chance?"

"Excellent, if the Prussian Guards arrive on time."

Both men had been silent for a moment,

knowing that actually the situation was very much more critical than it appeared on the surface.

"Good luck!"

Ivar Harling, turning his horse, galloped to where Wellington was watching the battle and saw that the Duke had ordered his Cavalry to counter-attack.

Then as he rode to the side of the great man, the Duke turned to his *Aide-de-Camp*, Colonel James Stanhope, and asked the time.

"Twenty minutes past four."

"The battle is mine! And if the Prussians arrive soon," Wellington said, "there will be an end to the war."

Even as he spoke, Ivar Harling heard the first Prussian guns on the fringe of a distant wood.

When luncheon was over, the Duke suddenly felt as if the house was very quiet.

He was used to having people moving incessantly round him, seeing scurrying Statesmen with worried faces trekking in and out of Wellington's Headquarters in Paris, hearing sharp commands being given at all times of the day and night, and dealing with endless complaints, requests, and reports.

There were also parties, Receptions, Assemblies, and Balls, besides the long-drawn-out meetings at which everyone seemed to talk and talk but achieve nothing.

There had, however, been interludes which

were tender, exciting, interesting, and very alluring.

The Duke thought cynically that now that he was who he was, these would multiply and he could come under a very different pressure from what he had endured during the years of war.

He was of course well aware that as the young General Harling, with many medals for gallantry, women had found him attractive.

Those who had congregated in Paris either for diplomatic reasons or just in search of amusement had, where he was concerned, seldom been disappointed.

While they had had a great deal to offer him, he had had nothing to offer them, but after it became known last year that he was no longer just an officer of the Household Cavalry but the Duke of Harlington, things had changed considerably.

Now he knew he was a genuine catch from the matrimonial point of view.

At the same time, alluring, exquisitely gowned, sophisticated married women would find it a "feather in their caps" to have him at their feet, or, to put it more bluntly, in their beds.

War heroes were of course the fashion, and every woman wished to capture for herself the hero of the hour, the Duke of Wellington, or if that was impossible then the second choice was inevitably the Duke of Harlington.

At times he found it difficult to prevent himself from smiling mockingly at the compliments he received or to suppress a cynical note in his voice when he replied to them.

It was his friend Major Gerald Chertson who had put into words what he had half-sensed for himself.

"I suppose, Ivar," he had said, "you know that as soon as you get home you will have to get married?"

"Why the hell should I do that?" the Duke asked.

"First, because you have to produce an heir," the Major replied. "That is obligatory on the part of a Duke! You must also prevent that exceedingly unpleasant relative of yours, Jason Harling, from eventually stepping into your shoes, as he is extremely eager to do."

"Are you telling me that Jason Harling is heir presumptive to my title?"

"I certainly am," Gerald Chertson replied. "At least he has been boasting of it lately, loudly and clearly all over Paris."

"I have never thought about it, but I suppose he is!" the Duke remarked.

He remembered that Richard Harling had not been the only member of the family to fall at Waterloo. Another cousin, the son of the last Duke's younger brother, had also died early in the battle, although it was not reported until three days later.

On the fourth Duke's death, in 1817, the title would have been his father's, had he been alive. Instead, it was his.

Now that Gerald spoke of it, he recalled that

17

the title would next go to another and more distant branch of the family now represented by Jason Harling.

He was the one relative of whom the Duke was thoroughly ashamed.

He had always been extremely relieved that during hostilities he had not come into contact with Jason.

They had, however, met in Paris after the war had been won.

The Duke thought Jason had always been an odious child, and he had grown up into an even more odious man.

He had seen very little of the war, but he had managed, by scheming and ingratiating himself in a manner which most men would think beneath them, to get himself a safe and comfortable post.

He became *Aide-de-Camp* to an elderly armchair General who never left England until the French had laid down their arms.

The way Jason toadied to those in power made most men feel sick, but it ensured that he lived an extremely pleasant life.

He managed to move in the best social circles, and he never missed an opportunity to feather his own nest.

The Duke had heard rumours of his accepting bribes and of other ways in which Jason took advantage of his position, but he had told himself it was not his business and tried not to listen.

Now as head of the family he knew that he

could not ignore Jason as he had in the past, and he had not realised that he was his heir should he not have a son.

Aloud he had said to his friend Gerald Chertson:

"If there is one thing that would make me look on marriage with less aversion, it would be the quenching of any hopes that Jason might have of stepping into my shoes."

"I have heard that he has been borrowing money on the chance of it," Gerald replied.

"I do not believe you!" the Duke exclaimed. "Who would be fool enough to advance Jason any money on the chance of my not producing an heir?"

"There are always Usurers ready to take such risks at an exorbitant rate of interest," Gerald remarked.

"Then they must be crazy," the Duke said angrily. "After all, I have not yet got one foot in the grave, and I am perfectly capable of having a family, and a large one!"

"Of course, it all depends on whether you live to do so."

"What are you insinuating?"

Gerald paused before he replied:

"I heard, but paid no attention to it at the time, that after Richard's death at Waterloo, Jason had a large wager that you would not be a survivor."

"Well, he lost his money," the Duke said sharply.

"I agree that you are now not likely to be killed

19

by a French bullet, but there is always such a thing as an — accident."

The Duke threw back his head and laughed.

"Really, Gerald, now you are trying to frighten me! Jason is far too much of a shyster to soil his hands with murder."

"I do not suppose it would be Jason's hands which would get dirty," Gerald Chertson answered drily. "Do not forget there was an attempt to assassinate Wellington in February."

"That is true. But André Cantillon was an assassin with a fanatical devotion to Bonaparte."

"I know that," Gerald Chertson replied. "At the same time — and I am not trying to frighten you — Jason Harling has a fanatical devotion to himself and his future."

"I refuse to worry about anything so absurd," the Duke said loftily.

However, as he walked from the Dining-Room towards the Library after an excellent meal, something struck him.

Together with his satisfaction with the house and everything which now had changed his life to a bed of roses from one which at times had been on very hard ground, he felt that Jason Harling was undoubtedly longing for his future to be assured.

"I suppose I shall have to marry," he told himself.

It was a depressing thought, and his mind wandered to the beautiful Lady Isobel Dalton.

She had made it quite clear when he left Paris that as she would be in London next week, she

20

expected to see a great deal of him.

The daughter of a Duke and widow of an elderly Baronet who had died of a heart-attack from over-eating and over-drinking, Lady Isobel was a very gay widow.

She had been one of the many women in Paris — French, English, and Russian — who had been eager to console the war warriors after their long years in the wilderness.

At every party they had glowed like lights in the darkness, and the Duke had found that Isobel's arms encircled his neck almost too eagerly, while her lips invited his even before he had any desire to kiss them.

However, it would have been impossible not to become aroused by the fiery delights which Lady Isobel offered him, and by the flattery with which she made him feel he was the only man in the world.

"I love you! I want you!" she had said a thousand times. "I loved you the moment we met, and now, dearest, you are in a position I never dreamt would be yours. I love you because you will behave exactly as a Duke should."

He was well aware that she pressed herself both physically and determinedly closer and closer to him, and when he had stayed with her after dinner the night before he left Paris, she had made her intentions very clear.

"As soon as you have everything in order, I will join you," she had said softly. "We will entertain and make our parties the smartest, the most fashionable, and the most influential in the whole of London."

She had given a little sigh before she said:

"The Prince Regent is getting very old, and the *Beau Monde* needs a new leader, and who would look more handsome and more dashing or authoritative than you?"

She paused, expecting the Duke to say that no-one was more beautiful than she was.

But he realised that he was being pushed into declaring himself, and he had not yet made up his mind whether he wished to marry anyone, let alone Lady Isobel.

When he thought about it, he knew it would be a marriage which would please his many Harling relations and be acclaimed as "sensible" by the Social World at large.

Although Isobel could excite and arouse him as few women had been able to do, something which he called his "intuition" told him she was not really the type of woman with whom he desired to spend the rest of his life.

He had learnt in the Army that women were for pleasure and should not encroach too closely on the man's world of living, fighting, and dying for his country.

Lady Isobel was very different from the attractive young Portuguese women who offered themselves to the tired men who needed some respite after the hard fighting in the Peninsular War.

She was different, too, from the attractive, cheerful little French *cocottes* who could make a man laugh, however tired he might be, and even find it a joke that they had picked his pocket just before he left.

But women were women, and while a man must sometimes relax from the hard realities of war, marriage was a very different thing!

As he had travelled back over Northern France and had an uncomfortable crossing on a tempestuous Channel, the Duke, when he was not thinking of his new possessions, found himself thinking of Isobel.

She was beautiful and confessed her love for him very convincingly.

Yet, there was something stronger than that thought, which he could not understand, and which held him back from asking the question that she was longing to hear.

"I must be with you, Ivar," she had said a thousand times. "I cannot live without you, and I know you would be lost and lonely without me."

It had been easier to cover her lips with his and kiss her than to argue.

The Duke had known when he left Isobel that she was closing up, before coming to London, the house in which she had been living in Paris.

It was part of a deliberate plan, because she was determined with a steel-like will which lay somewhere in that soft, seductive body, that she would become the Duchess of Harlington.

Thinking of her made the Duke feel restless.

He walked to the fireplace and dragged violently at the elegant needlework bell-pull.

He imagined the wire running down the corridor until the iron bell was jerked backwards and forwards in the passage outside the pantrydoor, where it was impossible for Bateson and the footmen not to hear it.

He did not have to wait long before the door opened and Bateson, rather breathless, appeared.

"I have changed my mind," the Duke said. "I have decided I will visit the Castle today. It should not take me more than two hours to drive there."

He saw a look of consternation on Bateson's face.

"Has Your Grace informed Lady Alvina of Your Grace's intention?"

"I meant to stay here," the Duke said, "at least until the end of the week, but I will see the Castle and return either tomorrow or the day after."

"I think it'd be wise for Your Grace to warn Her Ladyship of your arrival."

The Duke smiled.

"I expect I shall be comfortable enough, and after such a good luncheon I will not be very hungry for dinner. Congratulate the Cook, Bateson, after you have ordered the Phaeton and the new team of horses which I understand are already in the stables."

As he had no intention of arriving in England without excellent horses, he had asked Gerald, when he left Paris a week earlier, to go to Berkeley Square and see what horses were waiting for him.

"If they are not up to scratch," he had said, "buy me a team worth driving."

As he and Gerald shared a taste in horses, as in other things, he knew he would not be disappointed, and when twenty minutes later he was told that the Phaeton was at the door, he saw that his friend had done him proud.

The four chestnuts were perfectly matched. They were also exceedingly well bred, and he knew he would be able to cover the distance from Berkeley Square to Harlington Castle very quickly.

Unfortunately, at the moment he was not aware of what the record was, and as the groom who was to accompany him had also been engaged by Gerald, it was no use asking him.

Instead, as his trunk was strapped to the back of the Phaeton, he said to Bateson:

"I have told my valet to take the rest of the day and part of tomorrow off so that he can visit his relatives who live in London. I expect there will be someone who will look after me at the Castle."

"I hopes there'll be, Your Grace," Bateson murmured. "But I thinks it's a mistake, Your Grace, not to take your own man with you."

"Nonsense!" the Duke replied. "You are worrying about me unnecessarily, as you did when I was a small boy. I am sure the Castle will be just as I remember it."

He sprang up into the Phaeton and took the reins from the groom.

It was with a feeling of intense satisfaction that he looked forward to enjoying every minute of driving the finest team of horses he had ever possessed.

The Phaeton, which Gerald had also purchased for him, was so light that it seemed almost to spring off the ground as if it had wings on its wheels.

As he drove round Berkeley Square, he would have seen, had he looked round, Bateson staring after him with a look of apprehension on his old face.

He walked into the house and, as he did so, told the footmen sharply to wind up the red carpet which they had put down over the steps and out over the pavement.

Then he went into the kitchen, where his wife was clearing up after the luncheon with the help of two new scullery-maids who had no idea where to put anything.

"Has he gone?" Mrs. Bateson asked.

Bateson nodded.

"He's not to let Her Ladyship know that he's coming."

Mrs. Bateson put down on the table with a bang the heavy brass sauce-pan she was holding.

"We was told!" she said almost fiercely.

"Yes, I know. His Grace had meant to stay here, I understand, for several days, and we'd then have had a chance to inform Her Ladyship."

Mrs. Bateson gave a sigh.

"As it is, there's nothing we can do. I suppose

you didn't think to say anything to him?"

" 'Course not! It's not my place."

"He'll have a shock, of that there's no doubt!"

As Mrs. Bateson spoke there was a ring on the bell. Bateson got up slowly from the chair.

"Who can that be?"

"Caller, probably."

"I suppose I'd better go myself," Bateson grumbled. "These young 'uns won't know what to say."

He padded slowly back along the passage to the Hall as if his feet were hurting him.

As he opened the door, he saw to his astonishment that the Phaeton in which the Duke had just driven away was outside.

"What is it? What's happened?" he asked the groom who was standing on the door-step.

"His Grace has left in the Library some papers which he particularly wanted with him."

Bateson smiled.

It was somehow almost a relief to find that his new Master was human and could make mistakes like everyone else.

"Come with me," he said to the groom, and in a dignified manner walked across the Hall towards the Library.

The Duke, holding the reins of his team outside the house, was frowning. He could not think how he could have been so stupid as to leave behind the papers the Bank had sent him with an inventory of the contents of the Castle.

He supposed he had been so busy admiring

the house and its contents that it had for a moment slipped his tidy, self-disciplined mind, which usually made him punctilious about the smallest detail with which he was concerned.

However, he had gone only a short distance and little time would be lost.

It was then that he heard a voice. He looked down to see an elderly man with white hair and a somewhat lugubrious face looking up at him.

"May I ask, Sir, if you're the new Duke of Harlington?" he enquired.

"I am."

"I was a-calling to see Your Grace."

"I am afraid you are too late. I am just leaving. I will be back in a few days."

"It's important that I see Your Grace now."

"What is it about?" the Duke asked.

As he spoke he glanced towards the front door, hoping the groom would return and he could be on his way.

With a little hesitation the man said:

"It concerns certain family treasures. I have one here in which I think Your Grace'd be interested."

"Thank you, but I am not buying anything at the moment."

"It is not a question of buying it, Your Grace, but redeeming."

As the man spoke he opened the black bag he was holding in his hand and drew out a large silver bowl. The Duke looked at it indifferently, then noticed the crest engraved on the side of the bowl.

28

When he looked a little more closely, he was aware that it was an exquisite piece of silver-work which he was almost sure was by Louis XV's famous goldsmith Thomas Germain.

His mind went back to the last time he had dined at the Castle. He could almost swear the bowl had stood on the Dining-Room table between the candelabra.

His father, who was there with him, had remarked that there was no family in the whole country with such a fine collection of silver- and gold-work as the Harlings'.

"Where did you get that?" he said harshly.

Before the man could answer, the Duke added:

"If it has been stolen, you have no right to have it in your possession!"

"I've every right, Your Grace, as I can prove, should you be interested."

The Duke drew in his breath.

"I am interested," he said, "and I want a very good explanation or I shall have you taken in front of the Magistrates!"

The man did not seem unduly perturbed.

At the moment the groom returned, holding the papers in his hand. As he was about to climb onto the Phaeton, the Duke said:

"Hold the horses, I have to see this man before I leave."

As he spoke, he took the papers from the groom and transferred them to the inside pocket of his coat. Then he stepped down onto the pavement.

"Follow me," he said sharply, walking up the steps and into the house.

The man followed him across the Hall and into the Library, and Bateson closed the door behind them.

"Let me see that bowl again!" the Duke demanded. "What is your name?"

"Emmanuel Pinchbeck, Your Grace. I'm a pawn-broker."

"A pawn-broker!" the Duke repeated.

That was something he had not expected.

"Are you telling me this bowl was pawned?"

"Yes, Your Grace, with a great number of other things."

The Duke's lips tightened as he put the bowl down on the table. It was the most beautiful piece of silver-work he had ever seen.

"You had better start from the beginning," he said quietly but with a note of steel in his voice. "Tell me how you came into possession of this bowl. Who brought it to you?"

Without speaking, Emmanuel Pinchbeck drew out a piece of paper from his pocket and handed it to the Duke. It was somewhat soiled but he could read written quite clearly:

I, Emmanuel Pinchbeck, have loaned the sum of thirty pounds on a silver bowl circa 1690 and will keep it in my possession as long as the interest of thirty per cent is paid to me annually by the owner, who accepts the terms of this contract.

In an elegant, educated hand was the signature *Alvina Harling*.

The Duke looked at it and his chin was squared and his lips set in a hard line. He then said:

"How many other things have you besides this bowl?"

"Six small pictures, Your Grace, several miniatures, four more silver bowls, a snuff-box which is very elegant set with emeralds and diamonds, and two gold candelabra worth a good deal more than what they were pawned for."

There was silence before the Duke said:

"Why have you come to me?"

"I've come to you, Your Grace, because on hearing that Your Grace had inherited the title, I thought it would be to your advantage to redeem everything I hold."

There was again silence. Emmanuel Pinchbeck quickly went on:

"Frankly, Your Grace, I needs the money, and the arrangement isn't satisfactory to me as it stands."

"Why not?"

"Because thirty per cent is a good deal lower than other pawn-brokers charge, and I'm unable to sell what has increased in value, not because of their intrinsic worth, but because the price of gold and silver has risen."

"You mean they would be worth more melted down?" the Duke asked.

He spoke with a note of horror in his voice, but

Emmanuel Pinchbeck merely nodded.

"Yes, Your Grace. As I said, times are hard, and I can't go on holding all these things indefinitely."

"How long have you held them already?"

"Nearly three years, Your Grace. I'll never get my money back, and as I said, that's not satisfactory. Not satisfactory at all."

The Duke realised that he was serious, and there were beads of sweat on his forehead.

At the same time, he knew that the man was speaking the truth when he had said that thirty per cent was less than many pawn-brokers charged, and it was not satisfactory from his point of view to hold goods that he could not sell.

Because the Duke was a just man, he said:

"I realise that you have been extremely honest in not selling any of these things, especially those which you say could be melted down. I will therefore buy back from you everything that you hold which has come to you from the person whose signature is on this paper."

The old man's eyes seemed to light up and he smiled.

"I'm very grateful, Your Grace. I knew when I heard of your gallantry in battle that you'd treat me fairly and that I needn't be afraid to approach you."

"I am glad you did," the Duke said. "I will now pay you immediately what is owing on this silver bowl. I shall be returning to London the day after tomorrow, at the very latest, and I suggest you bring the rest of the things here to me."

"That's very kind of Your Grace."

"What is the final total on this piece?" he enquired.

Emmanuel Pinchbeck looked at him out of the corners of his eyes before he said:

"It's been with me for two years and two months, Your Grace."

The Duke made a quick calculation and drew from the wallet which he took from the pocket of his coat notes for well over the amount necessary.

He handed them to Emmanuel Pinchbeck, who swiftly put them away as he said:

"I'm extremely grateful to Your Grace. It'll be a weight off my mind and'll certainly make things easier for me financially."

"I shall see you in two days' time," the Duke said. "In case I am held up, send someone to enquire if I am here before you yourself bring the goods."

"I'll do that, Your Grace."

The Duke walked towards the door, and Emmanuel Pinchbeck, carrying the empty bag, followed behind.

Bateson was in the Hall, and the Duke said:

"You will find a piece of silver on my desk. Have it cleaned and put in the safe until I return."

There was a sharp ring in his voice and his eyes were cold as he spoke. Bateson looked up at him apprehensively, opening his lips as if to say something. But it was too late.

The Duke was out of the house, and, seating himself once again in the Phaeton, he took the reins from the groom and the horses moved off.

As he drove away for the second time, Bateson turned to Emmanuel Pinchbeck, who was watching him go, and said fiercely:

"Why did you 'ave to come here making trouble as soon as His Grace returned? Scum like you only do harm in the world!"

"I wanted my money," Emmanuel Pinchbeck replied defiantly. "You've no right to insult me. I've kept my word to Her Ladyship and have sold nothing, even though I could have got a good price for some of them."

"Get out!" Bateson said angrily. "If you'd any decency you'd have waited a little longer. But no, you pawn-brokers are all the same, grab, grab, grab!"

"That's not fair . . ." Emmanuel Pinchbeck began to argue.

But there was no-one to listen. Bateson had gone back into the house and slammed the door behind him.

As Emmanuel Pinchbeck walked away he could hear the bolts being drawn across the door and the key turned in the lock.

Then, as if to console himself, his hand went to his chest and he patted it.

There was a twisted smile on his thin lips as he felt the notes the Duke had given him.

Chapter Two

As the Duke drove out of London and into the countryside he grew angrier and angrier. With all the money his predecessor had when he died, a great deal must surely have been at the disposal of his daughter.

Why then should his Cousin Alvina have dealt with the pawn-brokers?

He could not imagine why she should need money, unless of course there was some man she was supporting of whom her father had disapproved.

The Duke thought cynically that he had a very poor opinion of most women's morals or sense of honour.

He had always, in the back of his mind, despised married women who were unfaithful to their husbands.

There was also something fastidious, or perhaps almost puritanical, in his make-up which made him dislike the idea that he was by no means the first of Lady Isobel's lovers.

He was quite certain, although she had never said so, that she had been unfaithful to her husband while he was alive, and she had certainly made the most of being free after his death.

It was all part and parcel of the pace set by the Heir to the Throne when he was Prince of Wales and his example had been accepted by the majority of those in Society.

When he thought it over, the Duke knew that, although it seemed impossible, he would want his own wife to be very different.

He had never really thought about marriage before. As a soldier, he had been quite certain he could not afford it.

But now he was in the position of being obliged not only to marry but to find a wife who would both please him and prove suitable as the Duchess of Harlington.

He was well aware that, although it did not always happen, the head of a great family was looked up to and respected in the same way as was the Chieftain of a Scottish Clan.

Before the Duke of Cumberland had defeated the Highlanders and the rule of law in Scotland was revised and restored, the Chieftains had the power of life and death over their Clansmen.

The Dukes of England certainly did not have that, but on their own Estates they were, in most cases, looked upon almost as if they were Kings, and their word was law.

'It is like commanding an Army,' the Duke thought to himself, and remembered how Wellington was admired, honoured, and loved by the men under his command.

He had also known in his Army-life officers who had such powers of leadership that those they commanded were ready not only to serve them but to die, if necessary, in obeying their orders.

He did not boast to himself of having that particular quality, although actually he did possess it, but he had been praised often enough for the fact that his troops were smarter, were finer fighters, and certainly were better disciplined than those in other Regiments.

Discipline had been the key-word in the Army of Occupation, when it had been difficult to keep soldiers who were not fighting from looting or bullying the beaten enemy and invariably causing trouble where women were concerned.

But now that task was over, and the Duke asked himself whether he would ever be able to discipline a woman or force her to obey him as he had managed to do so successfully with men.

He was quite certain that with Isobel it would be impossible, and he knew that she used the passion she aroused in a man as a weapon to get everything she desired, without exerting herself unduly.

His lips tightened as he decided that she would certainly not be able to do that with him.

Yet, he wondered, if it actually came to the test,

whether he would not be as compliant as her other lovers had been.

His thoughts then returned to the extraordinary behaviour of his cousin Alvina.

First, he tried to remember what she looked like, but he could not recall seeing her since she was a little girl of nine or ten years of age.

He had spent a great deal of his time at the Castle when he was very young because he and his cousin Richard were the same age.

He had very few memories of Alvina before meeting her at Richard's twenty-first-birthday party.

He remembered thinking then that there was a large age-gap between brother and sister.

But it had been explained to him that the Duchess had unfortunately lost two other children prematurely in the intervening time.

It had therefore been a triumph for the Doctors when the Duchess's daughter had survived. Alvina must by this time, the Duke calculated, be nineteen or twenty.

He wondered what she would look like. The Duke had been a handsome man, and he knew that the Duchess had been acclaimed as being outstandingly beautiful.

He actually found it hard to remember Alvina's face, because on that occasion he had been so amazed by the magnificence of the Castle and the extravagance of the festivities which celebrated Richard's coming-of-age.

Never, even in his later travels, had he seen

better or more spectacular fireworks, and he could remember the fantastic decorations in the Banquetting-Hall, which had been filled with distinguished guests.

The ladies had glittered like Christmas-trees with diamonds on their heads, their necks, and their wrists, and the gentlemen, all wearing their decorations, were not eclipsed.

Because the Duke of Harlington was of such importance, there were several guests of Royal rank present, besides nearly all the Ambassadors to the Court of St. James.

He remembered thinking that their gold-braided uniforms, jewelled decorations, and be-ribboned chests out-glittered even the splendour of a full Regimental dress like his own.

Richard had made an excellent speech that night but now lay buried on the battlefield of Waterloo, while he, a distant cousin, was to take his place at the Castle as the fifth Duke of Harlington.

Then as he drove on, having left the suburbs of London far behind, and now moving through the open country, the Duke's thoughts returned to Lady Alvina.

Once again he squared his chin and tightened his lips.

"How could she have dared to pawn anything so priceless as the Germain bowl?" he asked himself.

When the pawn-broker had mentioned that among the other things in his possession there were several miniatures, the Duke had stiffened.

The Harlington collection of miniatures was the most famous in the country.

Some of them dated back to the reign of Queen Elizabeth, and almost every Harling who had owned the Castle had added a miniature of himself and his wife.

The Duke recalled that they decorated the walls of the Blue Drawing-Room, and it had given him intense satisfaction, when he was in Paris, Vienna, and Rome, to realise that none of these three cities had miniatures that could rival the Harlington collection.

He had never expected to possess any one of them or even to have the pleasure of seeing them frequently. But just as the Harlings always believed that the Castle belonged to them as a family, so they thought of its contents.

On his way back from France, the Duke had known that the one thing he wanted to do more than anything else was to see the Castle, live in it, and make it the focal point of his new life.

"Harlington Castle," he repeated to himself, and knew that the name meant more than could possibly be expressed in words.

The way in which his father had talked of the Castle was one of his first boyhood memories, and it had always seemed to him to be inhabited by Knights.

When he had first read the tale of King Arthur and his Knights of the Round Table, he had pictured them living in a Castle that was exactly like the one to which he belonged by name and birth.

Later, it coloured every fairy-tale he read and every history-book he opened.

When he was taught about the Crusades, he imagined very vividly the Knights setting out to attack the Saracens from Harlington Castle.

Queen Elizabeth had stayed there on her travels round England, and she therefore had a special place in his mind because she had feasted and slept as the guest of one of his ancestors.

So it went on through his history-lessons, until, when in real life he was fighting against the domination of Napoleon, he was fighting for England, but especially for Harlington Castle.

Yet, in the moment of his personal victory, when it was now his, he had discovered that there was a traitor in the family, a woman who had dared to take from the Castle some of its most precious treasures to pawn them for money.

'I can only be thankful,' the Duke thought, 'that by some sense of decency, or was it perhaps fear, she has not sold what has been passed down from one Duke to the next.'

He remembered asking his father once, when he was a small boy and they had stayed at the Castle, whether the Duke felt like a King.

"I am sure he does," his father had said with a smile, "but at the same time, just as in the case of the King, the Palace is his only for his lifetime. The Duke must protect it and improve it for the next Duke who will come after him."

Ivar had found it a little hard to understand,

and his father had explained further.

"Each Duke in turn is a Guardian or Trustee of treasures which do not belong to him personally, but to the family as a whole. It is his duty not only to leave the Castle as he finds it but also to look after the family and see that they are cared for and do not want."

"He must have a lot to do," Ivar had replied.

"It is a very big task indeed," his father had answered solemnly, "and one in which we can thank God no Duke so far has failed."

From what he could remember of the fourth Duke, he had been an admirable head of the family.

Therefore, it seemed almost unbelievable that his only daughter should have stooped to stealing, for it was little else, the treasures to which generation after generation of Harlings had contributed, and had pawned them to a man like Pinchbeck.

"It is a miracle," the Duke said to himself, "that he did not sell them, although that might perhaps have been difficult."

He wondered what the Trustees had been doing who were supposed to look after such things.

He realised that because he had been abroad so long, he knew nothing about them or indeed who was in charge of the Estates.

He thought, not for the first time, that he should have come home for his cousin's Funeral and taken charge there and then. But the fourth

Duke had died in January 1817, and at that time he had been in Vienna.

He had been there on an important mission on Wellington's behalf, and therefore he had not heard of his cousin's death until he returned to Paris, where he received the letter from Coutt's Bank.

In it they informed him that as he was now the fifth Duke of Harlington, they enclosed a list of all the properties he had inherited and the monies which had been transferred to his name.

However, it had been impossible at that particular moment to go to England.

He had actually suggested rather tentatively to the Duke of Wellington that he should do so, only to be told that he could not possibly be spared.

There was in fact a tremendous row going on over the reduction of troops in the Army of Occupation.

In December of the previous year, Wellington had declared that a substantial reduction in numbers was impossible.

The next month, however, he notified the permanent Conference of four Ambassadors that his opinion had altered and a reduction of thirty thousand men would begin on the first of April.

This meant that an enormous amount of planning would be left in what Wellington described as "the very capable hands of General Harling."

On top of this, Wellington was negotiating the first loan to the French Government by Baring

Brothers and Hopes, and he was relying on Ivar Harling's support and persuasiveness, especially in getting the other Allies to accept the idea of a loan handled by British Bankers.

In fact, there was so much controversy and so many delicate negotiations going on that the Duke had realised it was utterly impossible for him to leave Paris, however important it was, from his own point of view, that he should deal with his problems at home.

He had comforted himself with the idea that everything would go on running as smoothly as it had when the fourth Duke was alive.

If there were problems, they could wait and he could deal with them later.

He therefore merely notified Coutt's Bank that he would return as soon as possible, and almost forgot that his own situation had radically changed as he coped with the hysterical French, the feverish hopes of *Madame* de Staël for a free France, and Wellington's unceasing demands upon him.

There had been no more correspondence from the Bank, and he had therefore imagined that everything was well, and that Lady Alvina, who was living in the Castle as she was the fourth Duke's unmarried daughter, would see to everything until he arrived home.

He now thought that perhaps he should have written to her and that he had been somewhat rude not to have done so, but he had received no communication from her or from anyone else.

44

Therefore, he had confidently believed that no news was good news and that that was what he would find when he arrived at the Castle.

Gerald Chertson certainly had done him a good turn in buying for him such an excellent team of horses which would get him there quickly.

Gerald had left him a note at Berkeley Square, saying that unfortunately he had to go home to see his father, who was ill.

He would, however, be back in London at the end of the week, and would get in touch with him immediately.

The Duke had been disappointed, since he had expected Gerald to be waiting for him when he arrived.

But Sir Archibald Chertson was old and very demanding, and he accepted that there was nothing else Gerald could do.

"As soon as I get back, Gerald and I will enjoy ourselves," he promised himself.

He then remembered Isobel.

As he thought of her he could almost smell the exotic and seductive perfume she always used and feel her clinging arms round his neck, her lips on his.

However, Jason or no Jason, he told himself, he was not getting married until he wished to do so.

What was more, he had every intention of enjoying himself as a Duke, the head of the family and a very rich man, before he settled down.

"I will see Jason when I return to London," he

decided. "I will give him a quite generous allowance on the condition that he behaves himself. I expect anyway I shall have to pay off his debts."

He was quite certain they would be out of all proportion, which would anger him considerably.

At the same time, it would be impossible for him to start off as the fifth Duke with a family scandal.

It was about four o'clock when he turned his horses through the impressive, gold-tipped wrought-iron gates which were flanked on each side with a heraldic lion, which was the crest of the Harlings.

The gates were open and he gave a quick glance as he passed through the Lodges on either side. He noticed that one of them was empty.

This surprised him, for he remembered the Lodge-Keepers, who wore special uniforms with crested silver buttons. They had always kept the gates closed but on hearing a carriage approach would hurry to open them.

If the passer-by happened to be the Duke himself, they would sweep their caps from their grey-haired heads with what seemed a courtly gesture, and in the background their wives and daughters would curtsey respectfully.

The Duke had thought it was very much part of the pageantry of the Castle, and he missed it now.

However, there was no point in stopping to enquire what had happened, and he drove down the long avenue of huge oak trees, which seemed even larger and sturdier than when he had last seen them.

Halfway down the drive there was the first sight of the Castle.

It was very impressive and so beautiful that instinctively, without thinking about it, the Duke checked his horses.

Standing on high ground above a lake, the Castle overlooked the gardens, the Park, and beyond that the rolling country, much of which was thickly wooded.

Originally it had been built for one of the feudal Barons who had been brought under submission at the time of Magna Carta.

But all that remained of the original Castle was a Tower which had been heightened and strengthened with castellated ramparts a century or so later.

Adjoining the Tower was now an enormous edifice, the centre of which was Elizabethan, while other parts were Restoration, Queen Anne, and early Georgian.

It might be a hotch-potch of architecture, but each century had contributed to the impressiveness of the whole Castle, which from a distance gave the impression of being not so much a great fortification as a fairy-tale Palace.

The afternoon sun was shining on the hundreds of windows, and silhouetted against the sky were statues on the roof which the Duke remembered vividly.

Between each one was an exquisite stone vase.

He had as a small boy climbed up to see them close to, and they had then seemed enormous.

But now in the distance they too had a fairy-tale quality that once again made him think of Knights in armour, nymphs rising from the lake in the haze that hung over it in the early morning, and dragons living in the dark fir woods and breathing fire at those who disturbed them.

Then abruptly, as if he had no wish to be fanciful or poetical at the moment, his mind came back to Lady Alvina and her perfidy in daring to damage anything so precious as the traditions of the Harlings, all of which were centred in this one great building.

As he drew nearer he noticed, again with a little surge of anger, that there were weeds in the gravel sweep in front of the great flight of grey stone steps which led up to the front door.

He pulled his horses to a standstill and said to his groom:

"The stables are round to the right of the house. Take the horses there. You will find grooms to help you."

"Very good, Your Grace."

The Duke handed him the reins, saying as he did so:

"I will send someone from the house to help take the luggage in through the back door."

The groom touched the brim of his crested top hat. The Duke alighted from the Phaeton and walked up the steps towards the front door.

This was the moment for which he had been longing and waiting. But now that he was here, he half-regretted that he had not informed Lady Alvina of his arrival.

Because Gerald had notified them at Berkeley Square that he was coming home, Bateson had been waiting in the Hall, and two footmen had run the red carpet down the steps and across the pavement the very moment the carriage which had brought him from Dover had pulled up outside.

But here there was no red carpet, and as he reached the door he saw that it was open and for the first time wondered what he would do if Lady Alvina was away.

He then told himself that it would not constitute any problem, because the servants would obviously still be there.

He walked into the huge marble Hall and saw that the stone statues of gods and goddesses were still in the niches, and the wide staircase with its carved golden balustrade was just as impressive as it had always been.

He felt he was being welcomed home.

He stood still for a moment, looking at the tattered flags hanging beside the beautifully carved mantelpiece.

They had all been won by Harlings in battle, and he remembered as a small boy being told where each one had been captured.

Agincourt especially had remained in his mind. He looked at the French flag captured then as if to reassure himself that it was still there.

He walked on through the quiet house, remembering well where each room was and what it was called.

At the top of the long flight of stairs there was on the left the Picture-Gallery, which ran the whole length of the house, and on the right were the State bedrooms.

These included Queen Elizabeth's room, Charles II's, and Queen Anne's, and at the end of the corridor was the Duke and Duchess's Suite, in which so many of his forebears, with the exception of himself, had been born and died.

He remembered that to the right on the ground floor was the very large Dining-Hall in which he had last eaten at Richard's twenty-first-birthday party.

Beside it was a smaller private Dining-Room which had been designed by William Kent, where the family ate when they were alone.

To the left, where he was moving now, was the Library with its first editions of Shakespeare and books that had been collected for centuries, making it one of the finest and most valuable Libraries in the country.

Successively on that side of the house were the Rubens Room, the Library, the Red Drawing-Room, the Green Drawing-Room, and the Blue Drawing-Room.

The Duke's eyes darkened with the thought of the last as he remembered that that was where the miniatures were.

He wondered why the place was so quiet, with no-one about.

He came to the first door, which opened into the Rubens Room, and found that the furniture was covered in Hollands, the shutters were closed, and the darkness smelt musty.

He closed the door and moved to the next one, which was the door to the Library.

Here there was a light because the windows were not shuttered, and as he walked into the room he had the impression, but he could not be certain, that everything looked shabby and, although it seemed incredible, somewhat dusty.

It was then that he was aware of another human being.

It was a servant, and she had her back to him and was dusting somewhat ineffectively with a feather brush the books on one of the higher shelves.

He watched her for a moment and realised that the feather brush, light though it was, was dislodging a great deal of dust.

He suddenly felt he needed an explanation and asked sharply:

"Where is everybody? Why is there no-one in attendance in the Hall?"

Although he had not intended it, his voice sounded in the room almost unnaturally harsh and loud, and the woman at the far end of it jumped as if she was startled and turned round.

She had a duster over her hair and was wearing an apron.

The Duke, walking towards her, said:

"Is Lady Alvina at home? I wish to speak to her." It was then, as two very blue eyes stared up at him, he had a sudden idea, although it seemed most improbable, that this was not a servant.

When she did not speak, he felt he should introduce himself and said:

"I am the Duke of Harlington."

The woman facing him gave a little gasp and then said in a voice that was barely audible:

"I thought . . . you were . . . in France."

The Duke smiled.

"On the contrary. I have arrived back today."

There was silence; and the woman stared at him as if she could hardly believe what she had heard.

Then at last, finding her voice with difficulty, she said:

"Why did you not let us . . . know, and how . . . could you have . . . stayed away so . . . long?"

It was then that the Duke realised to whom he was speaking, and he said:

"I think perhaps we should introduce ourselves properly. I am sure you are my cousin Alvina."

"Yes, I am," the woman answered, "and I have waited and waited for you until I had given up . . . hope that you would . . . ever return."

There was a desperate note in her voice that the Duke did not miss, and after a moment, and because he knew it was expected of him, he said:

"I must apologise if I have seemed somewhat remiss, but I had urgent duties in France, and the Duke of Wellington would not release me."

He almost despised himself for making apologies, and yet he had the feeling they were necessary.

As if he was determined not to remain on the defensive, he said:

"If you wanted me back urgently, why did you not write to me?"

"I did write to you when Papa died, but there was no answer."

"I never received your letter."

"I did not . . . think that was the . . . explanation."

"Then what did you think?"

"I did not know. I thought . . . perhaps you were not . . . interested. It was . . . stupid of me . . . not to write . . . again."

"I apologise not only for not receiving your letter but also because I should have written to you. I realise that now."

She did not reply, and he smiled.

"My only excuse is that I had really forgotten you had grown up, and I was thinking of you as the little girl I had last seen when I was here at Richard's twenty-first-birthday celebration."

As he spoke he thought it was tactless to remind Alvina of her brother's death, but she said:

"It was kind of you to write to Papa after Richard was killed, but he would not read . . . any of the letters he . . . received or allow me to . . . reply to them."

The Duke did not quite know what to say to this, so, feeling it might be somewhat embarrassing, he walked away from Alvina towards the window, saying as he did so:

"It was impossible for me to return before now. Now that I am here, I realise there is a lot for me to see and a great deal for me to learn."

"A great . . . deal," she said, and her voice seemed to falter.

The Duke told himself that she was afraid because of her behaviour in pawning the family treasures.

When he thought of them, his anger rose in him again, almost like a crimson streak in front of his eyes.

Yet, because he had disciplined himself to have complete control outwardly over his feelings, he merely said in a cold, icy voice:

"What I need to have explained, Cousin Alvina, is why you have dared to pawn some of the treasures in this house, which I thought any Harling would regard as sacred."

As he spoke he thought he heard a little gasp and told himself she was surprised that he had learnt so soon what she had done.

He turned round and saw that she had taken off the duster which had protected her hair and also the apron she had been wearing.

She was very slim, and now he could see that her hair was fair and somewhat untidy. But she looked very young, little more than a child, and certainly not the age he knew her to be.

She was standing very still, holding the apron and the duster in her hand, and she stared at him with an expression in her eyes which he knew was one of fear.

"I cannot imagine," he said sharply, "what your reason could be for behaving in such a dishonourable manner. And I want you, Cousin Alvina, to tell me the truth as to why you were in need of money and for what purpose!"

Once again his voice seemed to ring out a little louder than he had intended.

As she still stared at him, apparently finding it difficult to answer his question, his anger suddenly boiled over so that he said furiously:

"Were you trying to trick me because you had no wish to see me in your brother's place? Or were you providing for some man who had taken your fancy and of whom your father did not approve?"

He paused to say even more furiously:

"The pawn-broker, Pinchbeck, tells me this has been going on for nearly three years, ever since your father died, and I cannot imagine anything more underhand and deceitful than that you should behave in a manner which undoubtedly would have hurt and dismayed him had he been aware of it! It has certainly disgusted me!"

He finished speaking and waited, and then in a voice he could barely hear Alvina faltered:

"I . . . I can . . . explain."

"So I should hope," the Duke interrupted, "and it had better be a good explanation!"

Again he waited, and Alvina began to say in a choked voice:

55

"It was . . . because . . . Papa . . ." she stopped.

He then realised that she was trembling as if she could say no more and was unable to hold back the tears that had come to her eyes.

She then turned and ran away from him down the Library and disappeared through the door.

The Duke gave an exclamation which was one of exasperation and frustration.

"Dammit!" he said to himself. "Is that not exactly like a woman? They always resort to tears when they are caught out!"

He did not really know what to do now that Alvina had left him, but he thought he would have no difficulty in finding someone else he could talk to.

He looked for a bell, but there appeared not to be one. So he walked slowly back down the Library, thinking as he did so how badly kept it was and that there was undoubtedly a great deal of dust on all of the books.

The silver grate was almost black and obviously had not been polished for a long time.

He went out again into the passage which led to the Hall. There was still no-one to be seen.

He opened the door of the Blue Drawing-Room, only to see that, like the first room he had entered, it was shuttered and there were covers over the furniture, and again there was that musty smell.

"What the Devil is happening?" he asked himself.

He was just about to walk on farther when he

saw a man coming slowly towards him from beyond the Dining-Hall.

The Duke turned and walked back, realising as
he drew closer that the man had white hair and
was moving slowly because he was old. He
thought, although he was not sure, that he recognised his face.

Then, as they met halfway down the corridor,
the man peered up at him as if he found it hard
to see him.

"Good-day, Your Grace."

"What is your name?" the Duke asked. "I seem
to remember you."

"Walton, Your Grace."

"Yes, of course. You were the Butler here when
I was a small boy."

"That's true, Master Ivar . . . I mean Your
Grace," the old man said. "I were first footman
when you came as a child, and then Butler when
you stayed 'ere with your mother and father. A
fine, upstanding lad you was, too."

He spoke with warmth in his voice as old
people do when they reminisce over the past, and
the Duke said:

"I am glad to meet you again, Walton, but you
must tell me what is happening. There was no-
one in the Hall when I arrived."

There was just a faint note of rebuke in his
voice, and Walton replied:

"We weren't expecting Your Grace."

"Yes, I know that," the Duke said. "And I
know the war has made a great difference to

everything in England, but I did not anticipate finding all the rooms shut up."

"There were nothing else we could do, Your Grace."

"Why not?" the Duke enquired. "Surely you have servants enough to clean them?"

"No, Your Grace."

The Duke stared at the old man and then said:

"Perhaps it would be best for me to have an explanation from whoever is in charge here. I imagine that is Lady Alvina."

"Yes, Your Grace. Lady Alvina's been looking after everything since His Grace died."

The Duke now regretted having caused her to run away so hastily, and he said:

"Well, Walton, as Lady Alvina seems to have disappeared for the moment, perhaps you had better tell me what I should know."

As he spoke he realised that he could hardly stand talking in the passage, so he said:

"Which rooms is Her Ladyship using besides the Library?"

"The Library's usually shut, Your Grace," Walton said slowly. "Her Ladyship was dusting it as she was trying to find a book she wanted."

The Duke thought that would account for the dust and the way his cousin had been dressed.

"Where can I sit?" he asked.

His voice sharpened a little because he was feeling frustrated by the way every question he asked seemed to lead him nowhere.

"Her Ladyship's using the Breakfast-Room,

Your Grace," the Butler replied. "It's the only room we've open at the moment."

The old man preceded him very slowly to the small room which faced South where the Duke remembered breakfasting last time he had stayed at the Castle.

Only the gentlemen used to come down to breakfast, while the ladies had preferred to stay in the bedrooms or their *Boudoirs* and had not appeared until much later in the morning.

As Walton opened the door, he recognised the attractive squared room that overlooked the lake.

He remembered that the early-morning rays of the sun used to shine through the windows on the long side-board laden with silver entree-dishes kept warm with a lighted candle beneath each.

There had been at least a dozen different foods to choose from.

There had been a large circular table in the centre of the room, and the Duke could recall the big silver racks containing toast and a cottage loaf baked that morning in the kitchen ovens.

There had been scones and rolls fresh and warm, together with a huge comb of golden honey and jams and marmalades made in the Still-Room.

There was everything that a man's body could require early in the morning, and for his mind there were the newspapers, freshly ironed in the Butler's Pantry, set on silver stands opposite each place at the table.

He had been fascinated by all the luxury, and

he knew vaguely at the back of his mind that he had expected on his return to England to find everything as it had been then.

But the furniture of the room was entirely changed: there was now only one small round table in the window and a sofa and an armchair standing in front of the fireplace.

The long side-table on which the silver breakfast-dishes had been laid had been removed to leave room for a bookcase.

It was a very fine Chippendale piece, yet somehow it seemed out-of-place in this particular room, with its walls covered with paintings by English artists of the Seventeenth Century.

The Duke had noticed with a quick glance that had been trained to be observant that there was a work-box of English marquetry and a *Secretaire* which was covered with papers and with what he thought looked like bills.

There were some small portraits on the mantelpiece and on the side-tables, and there was also a larger one of Richard, painted by Lawrence, over the fireplace.

He had the feeling as he and the Butler entered the room that they were intruding, although he told himself that it was absurd to feel like that.

After all, the place was now his, and Cousin Alvina was certainly not welcoming him with any enthusiasm.

Almost as if he wished to assert himself, he sat down in the armchair beside the fireplace and said:

"Now, Walton, tell me what all this is about. Why is the house shut up? Why are there no footmen in the Hall? And why is Lady Alvina using only this room instead of one of the Drawing-Rooms?"

The old man drew in his breath, and then with a voice which seemed to tremble he said:

"I'm afraid Your Grace doesn't understand."

"I certainly do not!" the Duke said. "And while I think of it, there is one special question to which I want an answer. Why did you allow Lady Alvina to take the silver Germain bowl out of the safe and take it to London, with, I gather, a number of other valuable things?"

There was silence. Then the Duke realised that Walton's hands were shaking in the same way as Alvina's had.

As he could feel his anger rising, the Duke said:

"Tell me the truth. I shall find out sooner or later, and I want to hear it now."

"It's quite simple, Your Grace," Walton said in a quavering voice. "Her Ladyship had no money."

Chapter Three

There was silence for a moment before the Duke said in surprise:

"What do you mean, no money?"

Walton cleared his throat before he answered:

" 'Twas like this, Your Grace. There was no money to pay wages and pensions, or even to buy food."

"I do not believe it!" the Duke exclaimed. "My cousin left a very large sum when he died."

Walton looked uncomfortable before he said:

"I thinks, Your Grace, that the war upset a great number of people and His late Grace was one of them."

"You mean when His Lordship was killed?"

"Before that, Your Grace. Things began to get much more expensive, and His Grace decided to economise."

The Duke's lips tightened.

It seemed incredible, in view of the huge sum

of money he knew was in the Bank, that his cousin should have thought it necessary to economise to the point of considering the wages of his domestic staff.

He remembered now, although it had not occurred to him before, hearing talk of what was happening in England while he was in Paris.

Someone had told him that the Duke of Buccleuch, because of agricultural distress, had left his farm rents uncollected and was not visiting London so that he might have more cash to pay his retainers.

He had hardly listened to what had been said at that moment because he was more immediately concerned with so much that was happening in Europe.

Now he supposed that it had been foolish of him not to have made enquiries if at the Castle, like in other places in England, there were difficulties on the farms as well as the problem of unemployment.

He had read in the newspapers about unrest in the country, and politicians arriving in Paris from England had confirmed it, since wages had been forced down as thousands of ex-soldiers and sailors were released from the services.

There had also been no compensation or pensions for those who had fought so valiantly.

The Duke had put the information at the back of his mind, to be considered later when he returned home, but now he realised that it was an urgent personal problem which he had to face.

Yet, it still seemed incredible that Walton should talk of there being no money, when he knew how much there was available.

"Surely," he said aloud, "the Duke must have been aware of the difficulties, or whoever managed the Estate could have explained it to him."

"There was no-one, Your Grace."

"Why was there no-one?" the Duke asked sharply.

"His Grace quarrelled with Mr. Fellows, who had been in charge for thirty years, just before His Lordship was killed."

"And he was not replaced?" the Duke asked.

"No, Your Grace."

"So who has been managing the Estate?"

"Lady Alvina, and it's been very hard for her, very hard indeed, Your Grace. She had no money to pay the pensioners."

"I can hardly believe it," the Duke muttered beneath his breath.

Then, as if he felt that this was something that he should discuss with his cousin, not with a servant, he said:

"Who is here in the house at the moment?"

"There's just m'wife and m'self, M'Lord, and Mrs. Johnson, who I daresay you remember, who's been the Cook for over forty years, and Emma, who's getting on for eighty and can't do much."

"Is that all?" the Duke enquired.

"Everyone else was either dismissed on His Grace's orders, or left."

"It cannot be true."

64

The Duke was silent for a moment, then he said:

"Thank you for what you have told me, Walton. I think I must discuss this further with Lady Alvina. Will you ask her if she will join me?"

There was some hesitation before Walton said:

"I don't think Lady Alvina's in the Castle, Your Grace."

The Duke sat upright.

"What do you mean she is not in the Castle? Where could she have gone?"

Again there was a pause before Walton said:

"I thinks Her Ladyship were somewhat distressed, and I sees her leave, Your Grace."

"I do not understand. Where can she have gone?"

Again there was an uncomfortable silence before the Duke said:

"I am afraid I must have upset her, which is something I should not have done. Please tell me where I can find her."

He spoke in the persuasive manner which invariably enabled him to get his own way when more authoritative methods failed.

However, Walton shuffled his feet.

"I don't think, Your Grace, that Her Ladyship'll want you to find her at the moment."

"I can understand that," the Duke said quietly, "but you are well aware, Walton, having known us since we were children, that Lady Alvina is the one person who can help me to put right what is wrong and clear up what is obviously a mess."

He thought he saw the old man's eyes lighten a little, and then he said:

"Well, it's like this, Your Grace. If I tells you where Her Ladyship is, I'll be giving away a secret which His late Grace didn't know because he wouldn't have approved."

It flashed through the Duke's mind again that perhaps Alvina had some man in whom she was interested, but he merely replied quietly:

"I think you will understand, Walton, that whatever His Grace felt or did not feel about things, now that I am taking his place I shall have to make a great number of alterations. The first one is to restore the Castle to what it was in the old days."

He could not help thinking with some amusement that now he, of all people, was talking about "the good old days." Yet, it was obvious that if things were to be restored as he wanted, he would have to step back into the past for an example of how they should be done.

Still Walton hesitated, until at last he said:

"When His Grace was making economies he turned Her Ladyship's Governess, Miss Richardson, out of the Castle, and as she'd nowhere to go, Her Ladyship persuaded her to live in what had been the under-gardener's cottage."

"Why did she not have anywhere to go?" the Duke asked curiously.

"Miss Richardson's getting on in years, Your Grace, and she has rheumatism, which makes it hard for her to walk quickly or for any distance."

"So you think that Her Ladyship has gone now to Miss Richardson in the under-gardener's cottage," the Duke said as if he was thinking it out for himself.

"Yes, Your Grace."

"Very well, I will go find her."

He rose from the chair and walked towards the door as Walton said:

"Mrs. Johnson, Your Grace, was wondering, if you are staying tonight, what you'd fancy for dinner."

Perceptively the Duke understood that if he wanted dinner, it would be difficult for the servants to provide the sort of meal they expected him to eat, unless he was prepared to pay for it.

"Now listen, Walton," he said. "You have to help me get things back to normal, and I expect you will be able to find some of the old staff in the village or elsewhere on the Estate."

He saw Walton's eyes light up, and he said:

"It may take a little time, but I suggest the first thing you do is get help for Mrs. Johnson in the kitchen and two or three young men to assist you in the pantry."

He knew as he spoke that Walton was finding it hard to believe what he was hearing.

Putting his hands in his pocket, the Duke pulled out his purse, in which there were a number of gold sovereigns.

He then took from the inside of his coat a twenty-pound note, which he put down on the small table where he had laid his purse, and said:

"This will help you get what is needed immediately. Send Mark, my groom, to a farm or the village to purchase meat or whatever Mrs. Johnson requires for dinner. I suppose there are some horses in the stables?"

"Only two that Her Ladyship's been riding, Your Grace," Walton replied. "One's getting very old."

"Mark can ride one of them," the Duke said. "In the meantime, do what you can to improve things immediately, and there is no need to worry about expenditure. I will deal with that."

As he finished speaking and walked towards the door, he was aware that Walton was staring down at what he had left lying on the table as if he could hardly believe his eyes.

The Duke did not go out the front door, which was still open, but down the passage that passed the Dining-Hall and the small Dining-Room.

He then pulled open the baize-covered door which led to the kitchen-quarters.

He came first to the pantry, where he could remember as a small boy he had been given sugared almonds and other sweet-meats by Walton.

The huge safe was still there, and the table on which the silver was cleaned, and there was also the bed that folded up into the wall for one of the footmen who was invariably on duty at night to guard the contents of the safe.

Now everything looked very shabby. The walls were damp and in need of paint, and the floor looked as if it could do with a good scrub.

The Duke walked on past cupboards and doors which he did not bother to open and the narrow staircase which led up to the servants' bedrooms.

Then on his right was the huge kitchen, which he remembered had always been a hive of activity.

The scullions would be turning chickens and great joints on the spit, and Mrs. Johnson and the kitchen-maids would be at the stove. Brass saucepans, polished like mirrors, had hung from the walls while the freshly cured hams had hung from a cross-beam.

Now it seemed smaller to him and very empty, and there was only one old woman with bowed shoulders standing near a small fire.

For a moment he found it impossible to recognise the stout, apple-cheeked Cook who had made him gingerbread men as a small boy and later, when he was going back to School, huge fruit-cakes which had been the delight of his dormitory.

As he entered the kitchen she turned round, and he saw by the expression in her eyes that she recognised him.

"Master Ivar! Be it really you? You've grown into a fine man, there's no mistake about that."

"Thank you, Mrs. Johnson," the Duke replied. "It is nice to see you again."

He held out his hand and felt how cold her fingers were and realised how old and frail she was.

"Walton has been telling me," he said quietly,

"that things have been very difficult for you, but that is all over now. You shall have help the moment we can find anyone from the village to come to the Castle."

He heard Mrs. Johnson make an inarticulate little sound and went on:

"I am looking forward to having one of those delicious dishes you used to cook for me when I was going back to Oxford."

"That be a long time ago, Master Ivar . . . I mean, Your Grace."

"A long time," the Duke agreed.

"Things have been bad, very bad these last years."

She gave a deep sigh before she said:

"We'd all have died, every one of us, if it hadn't been for Her Ladyship."

"That is what Walton has been telling me."

"It's true, Your Grace. We'd have been turned away after all these years without a penny, and there'd have been nothing for us but the Workhouse!"

"Forget it now!" the Duke said. "Everything is going to be exactly as it was when I was a boy and there was no war to make us miserable."

"That's the right word — miserable!" Mrs. Johnson agreed. "With that monster in France killing all our young men, His Grace was never the same after His Lordship fell."

The Duke, feeling somewhat uncomfortable at having taken his cousin Richard's place, replied:

"Now we must only look forward, Mrs.

Johnson, and I want you to tell the groom I have brought down with me where he can go in the village to find food and help."

He smiled at her as he continued:

"Tomorrow we can make further plans, but for the moment the best thing to do is just to cope with tonight, and actually I shall undoubtedly be very hungry."

He knew that unless Mrs. Johnson had changed very much, this appeal would not go unanswered, and she said in a different voice:

"You'll have the best dinner I can cook for you, Master Ivar, but there's no pretending that I can do it without vittles."

"That I understand," the Duke said. "Leave everything to me."

He walked away, passing the huge larder with its marble slabs on which there used to stand big open bowls of cream.

He remembered too the pats of golden butter from the Jersey herd and cheese which was made fresh every other day.

Then there were sculleries, a very large Servants' Hall, the Housekeeper's room, the boot-room, the knife-room, and various other offices, before he reached the yard.

He did not stop to look round but walked on as he knew this was the quickest way to the stables.

As he expected, he found that his groom was the only person there and had just finished putting the horses into four different stalls.

He saw at a glance that the roof needed re-pairing and the stable itself was badly in need of paint.

The stalls were comparatively clean, and as he saw the other two horses in them he had an idea that the only person who could have cleaned them was his cousin Alvina.

He told his groom exactly what he had to do, and was pleased to find that the man Gerald had engaged for him was quick-witted enough to realise that there was a crisis and was ready to help in every way he could.

The Duke sent him into the kitchen to talk to Mrs. Johnson, then looked towards the end of the stables where he could see the roof of a house.

He knew this was the Head-Gardener's and opened on the back of the very large, walled Kitchen Garden, which was out of sight of the Castle.

It had always provided him and his cousin Richard with apples, peaches, nectarines, green figs, and golden plums.

He had the horrifying feeling now that it would look like a jungle, and he therefore walked past the Head-Gardener's house quickly.

On the far side of it, about fifty yards away, was a very small cottage.

He was certain that this was where one of the under-gardeners, perhaps the most important of them, had lived.

He was sure he was not wrong in recalling that when he was young there was an army of men working in the Kitchen Garden, on the lawns, in the flower-beds, and down by the lake.

When he reached the cottage, he saw that the windows were clean and the small garden between the gate and the front door was bright with flowers.

He walked up the small paved path and knocked on the door, which he noticed needed painting, although the brass knocker had been polished and so had the keyhole.

For a moment there was silence, then he heard the footsteps of someone who walked with a limp crossing the flagged floor. The door opened and he saw an elderly, rather distinguished, white-haired woman looking at him.

The Duke smiled.

"I think you must be Miss Richardson," he said. "I am the Duke of Harlington."

Miss Richardson made a little effort to curtsey, but it was obviously impossible.

She did not, however, open the door any wider, and after a moment the Duke said:

"I think my cousin Alvina is with you."

"She is, Your Grace, but she has no wish to see anyone at the moment."

"I think you will understand, Miss Richardson," the Duke said, "that since I have just arrived and found things are very different from what I expected, the only person who can help me is Lady Alvina."

As he spoke, he had the uncomfortable feeling that Miss Richardson was contemplating telling him to go away and shutting the door.

Then, as if she decided it would be a mistake, she said:

"Would Your Grace be gracious enough to wait a moment while I ask Lady Alvina if she is prepared to see you?"

She lowered her voice before she added:

"She is somewhat upset at the moment."

"It was my fault," the Duke replied, "but I had no idea before I arrived that the Castle would be so different from what it was when I last visited it."

The way he spoke seemed to sweep away a little of what had been an obvious feeling of hostility on the part of Miss Richardson, and she opened the door a little wider.

"Perhaps Your Grace would come in," she said. "And if you do not mind sitting in the kitchen, I will talk to Lady Alvina."

The door was so low that the Duke had to bend his head and once inside he could only just stand upright.

The kitchen was like a small box. However, it was spotlessly clean, and he thought that the walls must have been white-washed by Miss Richardson herself, or else, though it seemed incredible, Alvina.

There was a very primitive stove, a deal table, and two chairs. On one wall was a dresser which held plates, cups, saucers, and three china jugs.

The window was covered by some very old and faded curtains of a rich brocade which the Duke thought must at some time have hung in the Castle.

He sat down on one of the hard wooden chairs while Miss Richardson limped through a door which he guessed led to the Parlour.

Now he was sure that this cottage, like so many of the other workmen's cottages on the Estate, consisted of two rooms on the ground floor, the kitchen and the Parlour, with a scullery at the back, and there would be two tiny bedrooms up the very small, ladder-like wooden stairs.

It was all so primitive that the Duke felt it was an insult that anyone who was refined and educated, as Miss Richardson obviously was, should have to live in such a place.

Yet, if the previous Duke had turned her away, as Walton had said, and she had nowhere else to go, it at least constituted a roof over her head.

He could hear voices in the next room, although he could not hear what they were saying.

Then the door opened and Miss Richardson said in a quiet, controlled voice:

"Would Your Grace come in?"

The Duke rose and again had to lower his head to enter what he thought was the smallest Sitting-Room he had ever been in.

It was so tiny that there was only just room for two very ancient armchairs and a desk which looked as if it might have come out of the School-Room, with a small chair in front of it.

Again, the windows had curtains that had once been of expensive material, and the paintings on the walls were amateur water-colours.

These he suspected had been done by Miss Richardson's pupils, one of them of course being Alvina herself.

His cousin rose as he entered. He saw that she had been crying and her eyes were enormous in her small face.

Because she looked so woebegone and very young, the Duke suddenly felt he had been unjustly brutal, in fact, unsportsmanlike, to someone so vulnerable and defenceless.

As he heard the door close behind him he said, and his voice was very quiet and sincere:

"I have come to apologise."

It was obviously something she had not expected, and for a moment she looked at him incredulously, but she did not speak.

"How could I have known — how could I have guessed for one moment," the Duke asked, "that your father did not leave you with any money, and that the staff in the Castle should have been reduced to what it is now?"

As if she felt embarrassed, Alvina looked down, her lashes dark against the whiteness of her skin, and he suspected they were still wet.

"Let us sit down and talk about it," the Duke said. "There is so much I want you to tell me, and I can only ask you to forgive me for upsetting you."

He spoke in a way that both men and women found irresistible when he was being diplomatic, and as if she felt her legs could no longer support her, Alvina sank down onto the chair she had just vacated.

The Duke sat a little gingerly in the one opposite.

"Suppose we start at the beginning," he said, "and you tell me why your father would not give you any money when there is in the Bank a very large sum which I have now inherited."

"A large . . . sum?" Alvina asked in a voice little above a whisper. "Do you . . . mean that we are not . . . bankrupt?"

"Of course not," the Duke replied. "Your father died a very rich man. Surely the Solicitors told you that?"

"We have no Solicitors."

"What do you mean, you have no Solicitors?"

He felt that once again he was asking questions too sharply, and he added quickly:

"Forgive me, but I am completely bewildered as to what has happened, and there appears to be no-one but yourself who can tell me anything."

"Papa was so . . . sure that we were absolutely . . . penniless."

"Walton has told me that your father was not at all himself after Richard died," the Duke answered, almost as if he was making excuses.

"That was true," Alvina agreed. "At the same time, even before that Papa had become very alarmed. He kept on talking about economy, and I think perhaps he had always been very cautious where money was concerned. Only Mama insisted on making everything so happy and comfortable for us at the Castle."

"That is how I remember it," the Duke said, "and there were certainly no economies at Richard's twenty-first party."

"Mama planned that," Alvina said, "and when Richard was killed I was so very . . . very glad he . . . had enjoyed it so . . . much."

"I always think of him enjoying life to the full," the Duke said. "When we were at Oxford together he never worried about his studies, although he did quite well. But he took part in every sport, and no party was complete without him."

He saw the expression on Alvina's face and added:

"I saw him just before he was killed, and he was laughing then and made a rather facetious bet with me about the length of the war."

There were tears in Alvina's eyes, which she managed to control before she said:

"Had Richard come . . . home, things would have been very . . . different, but when he died . . . I think Papa . . . died too."

There was silence until the Duke said:

"Tell me what happened."

"As I have said, Papa was already making many economies before that, and afterwards, now that I think about it, he was not himself . . . almost like a stranger . . . and he refused to give me any money."

She paused, then said:

"I know you are angry with me for pawning all

those things, but I could not let the pensioners starve or go to the Workhouse. He would not pay the Waltons their wages or, even give me enough money to feed them."

The Duke was frowning as he asked:

"Surely there was someone who could have helped you, even though you had no Solicitors? Walton tells me that there is no Estate Manager, and what happened to the Trustees?"

Alvina made a helpless little gesture with her hands.

"One had died before Richard went to France, another lived until last year and was very old and deaf, and the third, Sir John Sargent, lives in Scotland and never comes South."

"So there was no-one to help you?"

"No-one. I thought of appealing to the family, but Papa had quarrelled with most of them, and when the rest no longer received the allowance he had always given them, they wrote him furious letters, which he refused to read."

The Duke put his hands to his forehead as if he found it hard to credit before he said:

"As you really had no money, I can understand that you did the only thing possible, but I am still finding it difficult to credit that in your position there was no-one who could have helped you."

"I thought and thought of everyone," Alvina replied, "but after Mama died, Papa quarrelled with so many people, not only our relations but everyone in the County. He refused to entertain and just sat reading the newspapers, hoping the war would end and Richard would come home."

As if she thought the Duke did not understand, she added:

"Richard was the only person who could have persuaded Papa to look after the people on the Estate and the family who depended on him. He also would have prevented him from dismissing all the old servants. Papa would not listen to me."

She gave a deep sigh and continued:

"He always blamed me because Mama was not very strong after I was born, and he had so much wanted me to be a boy."

Her voice trembled for a moment and then she said:

"After Richard was killed he hated me, because he had no son to inherit."

She did not say any more, and in some strange way the Duke could almost read her thoughts.

He knew almost, as if she had said it aloud, that she was remembering how her father had shouted at her to get out of his sight because she was alive while Richard was dead.

For the first time since he had come into the room, he looked at what she was wearing and was aware that her gown was worn and threadbare.

Although she may have deliberately worn something old because she had been cleaning the Library, he had the feeling that it was many years since she had spent anything on herself.

Almost as if she, similarly, could read his thoughts, she said as if he had asked her the question:

"I have not been able to spend anything on myself for years, and when my own dresses became too small for me, I wore Mama's. But as I had so much work to do in the house when Papa had sent all the servants away, I would have been almost naked had it not been for Miss Richardson!"

She glanced toward the door into the kitchen and went on:

"She mended my gowns and even made me a new one from material that had been bought when Mama was alive, to be used for muslin curtains."

She tried to smile as she spoke, but the Duke knew it was an effort.

"What gave you the idea of pawning the things instead of selling them?" he asked.

"I am not so stupid as not to realise that everything in the Castle is entailed," Alvina replied, "just as it is in Harlington House in London."

She drew in her breath before she said:

"To be honest, I went through the inventories very carefully, to find out if there was anything that could be sold, but I could find nothing."

"So you went to that man Pinchbeck. How did you hear of him?"

"I often think," Alvina answered in a low voice, "that there is no such thing as chance in life and that everything is meant."

"I have thought that myself," the Duke agreed.

"When Richard was at Oxford he had got into debt, and when he came home to ask for money,

81

Papa was in one of his bad moods and gave him a tremendous lecture on extravagance. He paid up, but Richard found to his consternation one bill he had overlooked by mistake."

Alvina's voice softened as she went on.

"He brought it to me and said:

" 'Look 'Vina,' . . . that was what he used to call me . . . 'I am in a mess and dare not ask Papa for any more, and these people are pressing me.'

"I had no money of my own then, for I was just a child, and then almost as if someone told me what to answer him, I said:

" 'I was reading a book the other day about some shops in London with three golden balls outside them, and Miss Richardson told me they were what are called pawn-brokers.'

"When I said that, Richard jumped up and said:

" 'How could I have been so stupid? You are a clever girl, 'Vina, and that is where my gold cuff-links, my gold watch, and quite a number of things I have of value will be resting tonight.'

"He kissed me," Alvina went on, "swung me round in his arms, and said:

" 'I have the cleverest sister in the world, and a very pretty one, too.' "

"So that is how you know of Emmanuel Pinch-beck," the Duke remarked.

"Richard told me," Alvina replied, "what he had managed to borrow on all his things, and afterwards, when Papa was in a good temper and gave him quite a large sum, he got them all back."

"Well, fortunately enough, you chose an honest pawn-broker," the Duke said. "Pinchbeck has not disposed of anything you left with him, even though he had been tempted to. As soon as I arrived this morning at Berkeley Square he came to see me."

"So that is . . . how you . . . knew," Alvina whispered.

"Yes."

"And it made you . . . very angry."

"Very angry indeed," the Duke said, "because I did not understand."

"And now you . . . do?"

"I can only apologise for misjudging you and for making you more unhappy than you must have been already."

She gave a little sigh which seemed to come from the depths of her heart, then she said:

"Now there is some money in the Bank. What do you intend to do?"

"I intend," the Duke said slowly, "to make the Castle look exactly as I remember it when I last saw you, but I am sure you will tell me that first we have to see to the pensioners, the relations, and anyone else who has suffered since your father, or rather Richard, died."

Alvina gave a little exclamation and clasped her hands together, and once more the tears were glittering in her eyes.

"Do you . . . mean that?" she asked almost in a whisper. "Do you really . . . mean it?"

"Of course I mean it," the Duke answered,

"but I cannot do all that has to be done, and quickly, unless you help me."

"Do you . . . really want . . . me?"

He smiled.

"You know the answer to that question, and, quite frankly, I do not know how to begin until you show me the way."

"I have written down in a book everything that I have spent," Alvina said. "You will see, when you read it, that it is not only the pensioners and relations who have suffered, but also the farmers and everyone else on the Estate."

The Duke looked puzzled.

"When the farmers could not pay their rents, Papa wanted to turn them out," Alvina explained.

"So you sold something and let him think the rents had been paid," the Duke said quickly.

She nodded.

"He also wanted to shut up the whole Castle and said that as he was bedridden there was no need for him to keep any of the servants except for his valet. All the rest could leave."

The Duke looked at her incredulously.

"And who was to cook and clean the house?"

"Papa said I could do that."

Seeing the size of the Castle, the Duke could hardly believe that what he was hearing was the truth, and he exclaimed:

"Your father must have been quite mad."

"I suppose he was," Alvina agreed. "He used to get into terrible rages with me simply because I was not the second son he had wanted."

As if the Duke felt it was a mistake for her to think about how the late Duke had hated her personally, he said:

"What happened to his valet?"

"He died two months ago," Alvina replied. "He was very old, and I think he just kept going for my sake and because, like the Waltons, if he left the Castle he would have had to go to the Workhouse or starve."

"I cannot believe it," the Duke said again.

He thought of the value of the paintings, the statues, the furniture, and all the other incredibly rare treasures the Castle contained.

Yet, because the last Duke had obviously been crazy, so many people in it had actually been near to death simply for want of food.

"Of course," Alvina said, "you can understand that I dared not repair the pensioners' cottages, which are in a very bad state, and I also could not increase their pensions, because I really believed, since Papa kept on saying so, there was no money in the Bank."

She gave a deep sigh and went on:

"But at least they managed on the few shillings I gave them each week, and Papa was not aware that the farmers were begging me every month to help them when they had leaking roofs, cow-sheds which were tumbling down, and implements which they had no chance of replacing."

"It must have been a nightmare," the Duke said sympathetically.

"It was," Alvina agreed. "Every time I took something out of the safe, or a painting from the wall, I felt I was a traitor and was betraying the family trust, but what was more important than anything else was to keep those who were alive from dying."

"Of course it was," the Duke agreed, "and I can only thank you, Alvina, for being clever enough not to sell those things which are specially precious both to you and to me and to all the Harlings who will follow on after us."

His praise brought a flush to her face and she said:

"Do you really . . . mean you can . . . afford to make things . . . right again?"

"I am not going to tell you how much money your father left," the Duke said, "because I think it would upset you, but I suggest we go back to the Castle and start to plan exactly what we shall do, starting from this moment."

Then as he rose to his feet, he had an afterthought and said:

"I think that as I am the new Duke, people in the County may want to meet me. So, if you are staying with me, which I insist you do, you must have a Chaperone."

He knew that Alvina looked at him in surprise, and he said:

"I am sure you will be able to persuade Miss Richardson to come back to the Castle and look after you and also forestall there being any criticism that you are not properly chaperoned."

Quite unexpectedly Alvina laughed. It was a very young and joyous sound, and as the Duke stared at her, she explained:

"I am laughing because everything has been so frightening, so serious, and so utterly and desperately miserable, that it never struck me for one moment that I was a young lady in need of chaperoning."

She laughed again before she said:

"Of course, Cousin Ivar, you are right, and I know Miss Richardson would be only too pleased to come back and leave this pokey little house in which she has been hiding from Papa."

"How could he have sent her away after she had been with you for so long?" the Duke asked.

"She was another mouth to feed, and Papa was quite certain he could not afford it."

The Duke swept away the frown from his face.

"Then I suggest we celebrate the new era we are opening at the Castle, and be wildly extravagant. When we get back, I intend to ask Walton if we have such a thing as a bottle of champagne in the cellar."

"Yes, there is," Alvina said, and now there was a lilt in her voice. "When Papa said Walton was to go, I was so frightened that he might bring in some strange servants who would work for nothing that I made Walton give me the keys to the cellar."

Her voice was serious as she went on:

"I hid them, having heard that the unemployed men wandering about the countryside could cause terrible . . . trouble if they . . . raided a place where there was . . . drink of any sort."

Now the Duke was definitely frowning again. He remembered the marauding bands of French deserters who had caused endless damage in France, and he asked:

"Are you telling me there has been rioting and thieving by the unemployed in England?"

"There have been terrible troubles," Alvina replied. "I do not suppose it was reported in the French papers, or wherever else you have been, but English ones have been full of little else."

She looked at him almost defiantly as she said:

"Do you realise that the men who fought for the freedom of this country, and who were, according to the Duke of Wellington, the finest Army England has ever had, were dismissed without a pension, a medal, or even a thank-you?"

The Duke knew this, but it seemed more poignant now that it was being expressed bitterly in Alvina's soft voice. Then she added:

"Of course they are resentful! Of course they are desperate! And what do you think has been happening to those who were wounded and lost a leg or an arm? They are dying of starvation unless they can steal, and no-one can blame them for their violence in doing so."

Almost as if it were his fault, rather than the Government's, that the soldiers he had commanded and who had fought so valiantly were brought to such a pass, the Duke saw the sumptuous banquets he had attended in Paris and other big cities.

Almost as if she were standing beside him he could hear Isobel's seductive voice thanking him for the orchids he had given her, which he realised had cost enough money to provide ten starving men with a good meal.

Before he could reply, Alvina said more quietly:

"Now that you are home, perhaps you will be able to make those in Parliament and at the head of the Services realise that as far as this country is concerned, peace is worse than war."

As the Duke finished what had been a surprisingly good dinner, waited on by Walton and two young men who had to be instructed *sotto voce* in everything they did, he sat back in his chair and said to Alvina:

"I have enjoyed my meal immensely, and I must not forget to congratulate Mrs. Johnson for remembering that her strawberry tart was always one of my favourite dishes."

"Mrs. Johnson has never forgotten anything about you or anyone else in the family," Alvina said. "When they knew that you were to be the next Duke, they were so glad that if it could not be Richard, it was you."

She took a sip of champagne before she went on.

"I think we were all terrified that it might be Jason."

The Duke was surprised.

"Do you know your cousin Jason?"

Alvina nodded.

"He came here to stay after Richard died, and I knew that as he was looking round he was thinking that with any luck, you would be killed too, and he would become the next Duke!"

She paused before she explained:

"He invited himself, and the manner in which he went from room to room, looking at everything and making, I thought, mental notes on their value, made me very . . . afraid."

"I can understand that," the Duke said. "I have always disliked Jason, and actually I was told just before I left London that he was raising money on the chance of succeeding me in the title before I produce an heir."

Alvina gave a little cry.

"You must be careful, very careful. I am sure he is a wicked, evil person, and he might murder you."

The Duke stared at her for a moment, then he laughed.

"You are talking nonsense. I am quite certain that Jason would not go as far as that, but my friend Gerald Chertson actually warned me he would do anything to further his ambitions."

"I am sure he is absolutely ruthless where his ambitions are concerned."

"How can you be so positive?"

"Perhaps it is because I have been so much alone here. You will think I am over-imaginative," Alvina replied, "but ever since I was a child, I have had instincts about people and I am never mistaken."

"You mean you are clairvoyant?" the Duke asked almost mockingly.

"Not exactly," Alvina answered, "but you know that the Harlings are a very mixed breed and our Celtic blood is very strong."

The Duke raised his eye-brows as she explained:

"My grandmother was Irish, my great-grandmother was Scottish, and actually Mama had a great number of Welsh relations, although I have never met them."

"If it comes to that," the Duke said, "my great-grandmother was Scandinavian, which is why I was christened 'Ivar.' "

"So you are perceptive, too."

"I like to think I can judge a man without having to read references about him, and that if I follow my instinct where he is concerned, I am invariably right."

"And you can do the same with women?"

"If I answer 'yes,' you will be able to retort that I was completely wrong in the way I judged you."

"Did you . . . really think I had taken that . . . money for . . . myself?" Alvina asked in a low voice.

"To be honest, I thought you might be giving it to some man you fancied and of whom your father did not approve."

Alvina laughed.

"That was certainly very far from the mark! I do not think I have seen a young man for years. When Papa decided we were so hard-up that we could not entertain, he refused every invitation he received, and if anyone called, they were sent away . . . usually rudely."

"It must have been very lonely for you," the Duke said sympathetically.

"It would have been much worse if I had not had books to read and dear Miss Richardson to talk to."

She looked at the Duke, and then as she thought he might contradict her, she said:

"She is a very exceptional person. Her father was an Oxford Don who wrote several books on Roman history which were acclaimed by every scholar in the country. The fact that she was capable of helping him with them shows that had she been a man, she would undoubtedly have been an outstanding scholar."

"You were very well taught, then," the Duke said.

"Of course I was," Alvina said, "and thank you for asking her back here. She is very thrilled at the invitation."

"You did ask her to dine with us tonight?" the Duke said quickly.

"I did, but she declined as her legs were paining her so much as they often do at night-time, and when she is in pain she prefers to be alone."

"I see," the Duke said. "We must get someone who specialises in rheumatism, or whatever she has, to see her."

"Do you mean that?"

"There must be some Physician in London," the Duke replied, "who has studied the rheumatic diseases which affect so many older people."

Alvina put her hand palm upwards on the table.

"How . . . can you . . . be . . . so kind?" she said in a low, broken voice.

The Duke put his hand over hers. He could feel her fingers quiver almost as if he held a small bird in his grasp.

"I hated you," Alvina said in a low voice, "first because you had taken Richard's place and then because you did not answer my letter."

"I can understand that," the Duke said quietly.

"And then you were angry with me when you came here and I thought you were heartless and indifferent."

Her fingers tightened beneath his and she said:

"Now I am sorry I thought that."

The Duke smiled.

"I think our Celtic instincts have broken down or gone on strike. They were certainly not working efficiently when we first met each other! That is why, Alvina, we have to start again."

"We have started already," Alvina said. "Mrs. Johnson has three girls in the kitchen, and Walton told me before dinner that he had another footman coming tomorrow from the village and other people who used to be in service here with the Harlings for years."

Her fingers tightened again. Her eyes seemed

to glow, partly because there were tears in them, and she said in a voice that was very low:

"Thank you, thank you, for being exactly the head of the family we want."

Chapter Four

Driving back to London, the Duke knew that, if he was honest, he had never enjoyed two days more.

Alvina had taken him round the Estate, both of them riding horses from the team that Gerald had bought him, which were not only perfectly broken as carriage-horses but excellent to ride.

After the old and somewhat indifferent horses which were all that Alvina had after her father had disposed of the stable, it was, the Duke realised, a thrill for her to be mounted on such perfect horse-flesh.

He also realised that she rode extremely well, and because she was so happy she looked, he thought, exceedingly attractive.

Her habit was old and worn but had once been well cut, and because she had really grown out of it, it revealed her very slim and very elegant figure.

The Duke had ridden with many beautiful women in Paris when it had been fashionable to appear every morning in the *Bois*, and also in Vienna with the alluring, auburn-haired Beauties who prided themselves on their horsemanship.

Nevertheless, he thought that his cousin could hold her own from an equestrian point of view.

The fact that she was excited by what he was planning to do made her face glow with a radiance which he seldom saw in a woman's face unless he was making love to her.

They had sat up quite late last night, poring over the book in which Alvina had set down all of her expenditures since 1814 when her father first began cheese-paring.

At first, she had merely supplemented what she was given to pay for the food from what had been her dress allowance and from two hundred pounds which her mother had left her on her death.

Then, when her father became more determined that they were going bankrupt, she had started to pay the wages of the older servants whom he insisted must be dismissed.

However, he was by then confined to his bedroom and had no idea that they were still in the house.

"The Waltons, Mrs. Johnson, and Emma were all too old to leave," Alvina said in her soft voice, "but some of the younger ones found other jobs. The footmen had to go onto the land or into the Services and they were very bitter at being turned away."

She sighed as she explained:

"They had lived on the Estate all their lives, and their families had always served the Harlings."

"We can only hope," the Duke replied, "that some of them will be able to come back now."

"It was kind of you to arrange for Mark to take the Waltons and Mrs. Johnson in a carriage to the village."

"They could hardly walk."

Knowing the drive was over a mile long, Alvina gave a little laugh.

"It would certainly have taken them a very long time, and that of course was another reason why it was impossible for them to leave us even if they had wanted to, because Papa thought he had sold all the horses."

"But you managed to keep two," the Duke stated.

"I kept the one I had ridden for years," Alvina replied, "and poor old Rufus, whom no-one would buy. He must be over seventeen years old."

The Duke made no comment because, as he had said so often, what had happened seemed so incredible that now he was just prepared to listen.

He wanted, however, to find out and see for himself exactly what had happened.

When they visited the farms he could understand that no-one with even a shred of decency in them would have turned away the Hendersons because they could not pay their rent.

There had been five generations of Hendersons farming that particular farm, and on other farms it was much the same story.

He was really appalled at the condition that the farms were in. The roofs had not been repaired for years, and many of the outbuildings had collapsed altogether.

"Things were good in the war, Your Grace," one farmer told him, "but soon as it were over, no-one wanted the farmers any longer, and the big harvest of 1815 flooded the market."

The Duke was quick to understand that few farmers had saved money, and, being able to visualise anything but rising prices, they had invested everything they had in their land.

The poor soils they had ploughed in response to the war-time demand became economically unworkable when wheat prices fell disastrously.

By the time he and Alvina had ridden over only half of the Estate and listened to the despair the farmers expressed, he could sympathise with, although he certainly did not condone it, the fear which had made the last Duke believe he was ruined.

By the mercy of Providence he could repair much of the damage, but he could not help remembering that he could not replace the men who had been killed in battle and who would never return.

He had, however, told his own tenant-farmers that he would lend them money to make improvements without interest for three years, and he also promised he would find out when he returned to London what were the best markets available for the crops they grew.

Their gratitude was pathetic, and as the Duke and Alvina rode away from the fourth farm they had visited, he said to her:

"I hope that I am not being too optimistic and that there will be purchasers for the wheat, oats, barley, and all the other crops."

"What is more important than anything else," Alvina replied, "is that there should be work for the younger men."

The Duke knew this was true.

As he drove back to London, he saw in the villages through which he passed men who looked unmistakably as if they should be wearing a uniform.

They were sitting about on the Village Green or lounging outside the Inn, obviously with time on their hands because they were unemployed.

He thought to his satisfaction that at least he had a great number of vacancies now at the Castle.

The Head-Gardener was too old and too infirm to do anything active, but Alvina was certain that he would be able to direct any men they employed and would be aware of what would grow best in the Kitchen Garden.

He would also know where the strawberry-beds, the peas, the beans, and the carrots had been planted in the past.

The Duke had thought that the first thing he

should do was to find and engage an Estate Manager.

But because Alvina was so involved in this herself and he knew it would make her happy to re-employ those who had been dismissed, he had thought that could wait until she found it too much for her.

At the same time, the Estate was a very extensive one.

The next day they had visited other farms, inspected an Orphanage which had been closed for three years, and called at the Schools, which were empty and neglected.

There were also several Churches which were either on the verge of falling down or had no incumbent because the reigning Duke was responsible for his stipend.

When they returned to the Castle late in the afternoon, having had luncheon at a village Inn consisting of fresh bread and cheese washed down with home-brewed cider, the Duke actually felt quite tired.

Alvina, however, despite her frail appearance, seemed to be as fresh and as buoyant as she had been in the morning.

He knew she was stimulated and excited by the knowledge that the burden of misery and despair which had rested on her shoulders for so long had now been lifted.

It was after dinner, when it was getting late and they had almost completed their plans for the next few months at any rate, that the Duke had said:

"Now, Alvina, I think we will talk about you. You have set my feet on the right path, so I must do the same for you."

"What do you mean?" she asked.

"I think I am right in thinking that you are nineteen," the Duke said, "and you should have made your début in London last year, but of course you were in mourning. Now, with Berkeley Square at your disposal, you must meet the *Beau Monde* and, of course, the Prince Regent."

He expected Alvina to be excited at the idea, as he thought any young woman would have been, but to his surprise she looked away from him to say:

"I would much rather stay here. I am too . . . old to be a . . . débutante."

"That is untrue," he said. "And although I am very grateful for your help, I cannot allow you to waste your youth and your beauty tending old pensioners and opening Schools for obstreperous children."

Alvina had risen from the chair in which she had been sitting and walked across the Morning-Room to pull aside the curtains over the window.

Outside, it was night. The sky was bright with stars and there was a moon rising over the tops of the oak trees in the Park.

She stood looking out in silence.

The Duke, watching her, thought how slim and exquisite she looked in a white muslin gown which he knew had been made for her by Miss Richardson.

The muslin, which had been intended for curtains, revealed the soft curves of her breasts, but he knew she was in fact too thin, which doubtless was caused by not having enough to eat.

He had learnt that their staple fare had been rabbits which Alvina had paid boys from the village to snare in the Park, and eggs which came from a few old chickens that were cooped up outside the kitchen-yard.

The vegetables, the Duke learnt, had grown untended in the Kitchen Garden but had naturally become more and more sparse as the years went on, so that Alvina had to search for them amongst the weeds.

Because these were such an important part of their diet, she had planted potatoes to supplement what was growing more or less wild.

The Duke wondered why she was not more enthusiastic about the idea of going to London. Then suddenly she turned from the window to say:

"No! It would be a mistake, and if you do not . . . want me here, perhaps you would let me . . . live in one of the . . . cottages. I would be quite happy if Miss Richardson would . . . stay with me."

The Duke stared at her and found it hard to believe what she was saying, before he replied:

"My dear child, Miss Richardson is already an old woman, while you are young, very young, and your whole life is in front of you. Of course you must take your proper place in Society as you would have done had your mother been alive."

"Are you saying in a tactful manner that you . . . wish to be . . . rid of me?" Alvina asked. "Perhaps you are . . . thinking of getting . . . married."

There was just a little pause before the Duke said firmly:

"I have no intention of getting married, not at any rate for a long time."

He knew as he spoke that it was impossible to imagine Isobel caring for the people on the Estate as Alvina had done, nor would she wish, he knew, to spend any length of time at the Castle.

She would want to be at Berkeley Square, entertaining for the sophisticated, witty, pleasure-loving Socialites who were an intrinsic part of her life wherever she might be.

"If you do not . . . mind my being here," Alvina said, "please, can I stay . . . with you? I should feel . . . afraid anywhere else. You must be aware how . . . ignorant I am of the . . . Social World."

"It consists of people," the Duke replied with a smile, "people like you and me, Alvina, and they are not really a race apart, whatever you may have heard about them."

As he spoke, he thought that was not quite true.

No-one could be more different from the people in the cottages and the villages, who he had realised today almost worshipped Alvina, then the gay, irresponsible *Beau Monde*, who

103

were selfish, extravagant, and concerned only with their incessant search for amusement.

They would merely find Alvina a badly dressed country girl.

Because the Duke had spent what free time he had with the most exquisitely gowned Beauties in every Capital he had visited, he was well aware how important clothes were to women.

He said now to Alvina:

"You will have to go to London for one thing, if nothing else — to buy yourself new clothes."

He spoke without thinking that it might sound an insult, and seeing a flush appear on Alvina's face he added:

"Perhaps I should have told you before that you are very lovely, but even the most beautiful picture needs the right frame to show it off."

"I have a feeling," Alvina said slowly, "that you are flattering me to get your own way. I am not used to compliments and so I am suspicious of them. Although I would love some new clothes, I am afraid if I move away from here you will never let me come back."

She spoke lightly, the Duke was aware, but there was undoubtedly a quiver of fear beneath the surface.

"I promise you," he said quickly, "that the Castle is your home for as long as you wish to stay here."

"If you . . . marry . . . what then?"

"I have no intention of marrying," the Duke

said almost irritably. "At least not for a very long time."

"But you will have to, otherwise Cousin Jason will know he has a chance of taking your place."

"I will deal with Jason myself when I reach London," the Duke said, "and there is no need for you to worry about him any longer."

He spoke with a hint of laughter in his voice, then in a different tone he said:

"For God's sake, stop thinking of everyone but yourself. You have done that for far too long. I can assure you it is quite unnatural for a pretty and very attractive young woman."

He saw the colour come into her cheeks from his compliment, and she turned away to say almost obstinately:

"I do not . . . wish to go to . . . London."

"That is what you are going to do," the Duke said. "I suppose you realise that now that your father is dead, I am not only head of the family but also your Guardian, and you have to obey me."

She turned to look at him, and now there was a hint of mischief in her eyes as she said:

"And if I do . . . not?"

"Then I shall think of some horrendous punishment which will bring you to heel."

"And what will that be?"

"I cannot think for the moment," the Duke replied, "but perhaps I shall cancel the horses I intended to buy at Tattersall's for you to ride, or perhaps, worse, I will forget my plans for the Ball I want to give here in the Castle to introduce not only you to the County and to my friends from London but also myself."

"A Ball?" Alvina repeated almost stupidly.

"A Ball," the Duke said firmly. "And one thing is very important, Alvina, and that is that you should learn to dance gracefully the new waltz which was introduced to London by the Princess de Lieven."

Alvina came from the window to sit down opposite him on the sofa.

"Did you . . . really say a . . . Ball?" she asked. "I think I am . . . dreaming."

"I have every intention of celebrating my home-coming in a spectacular manner."

Actually he had not thought of it until that moment, but he knew that was much the best way to get Alvina involved in the world that he knew was waiting for her outside the Castle after the years of what was virtually imprisonment.

"I would never have thought," she said, "though Mama talked of it when I was very young, that there would ever be a . . . Ball in the Castle and that I could . . . dance at it."

"It is something I intend to give," the Duke said.

"But the Ball-Room has not been . . . used for . . . years. The walls all want . . . washing down, the floor . . . polished, and I am certain the mice have eaten holes in the . . . chairs and the . . . curtains."

"As I intend to give the Ball in a month or six weeks' time," the Duke said, "you will have to get busy."

Alvina gave a little scream.

"That is . . . impossible! Quite . . . impossible with . . . everything else!"

"Nothing is impossible when one has unlimited money, Alvina, and as you pointed out to me yourself, there are hundreds of men whom we know and can trust, because they are our own people, longing for work."

"Yes . . . yes, of course . . . that is . . . true," Alvina agreed. "But I have to try and . . . visualise how it can . . . possibly be . . . done."

"I am sure I can leave it in your hands," the Duke said, laughing, "and when I return from London in two or three days' time, I shall have found out which are the best dressmakers for you to visit, and will make arrangements for you to come to London with Miss Richardson and stay at Berkeley Square."

"You are going . . . too fast," Alvina protested. "I have already said that I have . . . no wish to be a . . . débutante."

"You can call yourself what you like," the Duke replied, "but just as I have my duties which are obligatory, as you are well aware, as your father's daughter you have yours."

This was irrefutable, and after a moment Alvina said in a very small voice:

"I know you are . . . right, but I am . . . sure I shall make a . . . mess of it all."

"Just as you are helping me not to make a mess of my inheritance, of which I have already admitted I am confoundedly ignorant," the Duke said, "I will prevent you from making a mess of what is waiting for you in London, and of that I am considerably knowledgeable."

They went on talking for a little while of what they must both do, apart from improving the conditions on the Estate.

Only when they walked upstairs side by side and paused on the landing to say "good-night" as they went in opposite directions did Alvina say:

"You are quite . . . certain that I shall . . . not be completely out-of-place in London and that you will not be . . . ashamed of me?"

"I am quite prepared to bet a considerable amount of money," the Duke replied, "that you will not only be surprised at your success, but in a very short time will begin to think of it as your right."

Alvina gave a little laugh, and he went on:

"You will then, like all women, undoubtedly complain and reproach me for the omissions in your programme for which I am responsible, and forget to thank me."

He was teasing her, but when Alvina looked up at him wide-eyed, she said:

"How could I ever be anything but very . . . very grateful . . . to you? Perhaps one day I shall be able to find a way to thank you."

Then, as if she felt shy, she said hastily before he could speak:

"Good-night, Cousin Ivar."

Then she slipped away from him down the passage towards her bedroom.

'I will make her a success,' the Duke thought. 'She certainly deserves it after all she has been through.'

At the same time, he could understand that the social life he was visualising for her was very different from what she had known previously.

It must have been very restricting for her to live alone at the Castle with her father, who had undoubtedly been mad, and after his death to be left with the fear of starvation and with no-one to advise her as to what she should do.

"It is all my fault," the Duke told himself for the hundredth time. "I should have come back, however much it annoyed Wellington."

But it was impossible to put back the clock, and now he knew his first duty as head of the family was to ensure, after all she had suffered, that Alvina's future would be very different from what it had been in the past.

When he arrived at Berkeley Square, it was a pleasure that lifted his heart to find Bateson and four footmen in well-fitting livery waiting for him and the Drawing-Room open, cleaned, and polished.

Actually, the whole house seemed to smell of bees'-wax.

The Duke had sent a groom to London the day before to warn Bateson of his arrival. The man was middle-aged, and Alvina had said that he had worked at the Castle before he joined the Navy.

He had then returned home to find time heavy on his hands because there was nothing for him to do.

The Duke, using his instinct, was sure that the man was trustworthy and good with horses.

He therefore engaged him immediately and told him to look round locally to find two other grooms whom he would recommend as men he would be willing to work with.

He had known by the way the man squared his shoulders and seemed to grow taller that he had given him back his self-respect after three years of idleness.

When he had sent him to London, he was certain that the instructions he gave him would be punctiliously carried out.

In fact, as soon as he entered the Drawing-Room, Bateson said to him:

"Major Chertson called this morning, Your Grace, to say that he had received your note and would be delighted to have luncheon with you today."

The Duke looked at the clock, and realising there would be three-quarters-of-an-hour before Gerald arrived, he decided there were quite a number of things he could do while he waited.

By the time Gerald Chertson appeared, he had written a pile of letters which lay on his desk in the Library. Some of them were to be delivered by hand and some were to be posted.

Gerald came hurrying into the room, and as the Duke rose to meet him he felt that almost a

century had passed since they had last talked together, before he had set off for the Castle, furiously angry because of what he believed to be his
cousin Alvina's treacherous behaviour.

He told Gerald all about it while they drank a
glass of champagne before going in to luncheon.

Then in front of Bateson and the footmen they
discussed mostly the improvements necessary on
the Estate and the horses he wanted to buy at
Tattersall's.

"I always knew you were a good organiser,"
Gerald said after the Duke had talked for a long
time, "and as you appear now to have a cam-
paign of your own on your hands, I can imagine
that it will not only give you pleasure but will be
very good for you."

"What do you mean by that?" the Duke enquired.

"I often thought when we were in Paris that
you were too comfortably in the saddle as the
great man's special envoy, with the red carpet
rolled out before you wherever you went, and you
did not have to fight for what you wanted."

"Fight? I have done damn little else for the
past nine years," the Duke said.

"I do not mean that sort of enemy, you fool,"
Gerald replied. "I mean fighting for yourself and
getting what you need personally, which is a very
different thing."

"I suppose you are right," the Duke agreed. "I
do not see very much difference, except that it is
rather like starting with a lot of raw recruits and

wondering if they will ever turn into the excellent soldiers you want them to be."

"You will do it," Gerald said, "but I am intrigued about this cousin of yours. Tell me about her."

The servants had now left the room, and the Duke said:

"That is where I am going to need your help. You have been in London far more than I have, and you are of course very knowledgeable as to what she should and should not do."

"Before you go any further," Gerald said, "you will have to find her a Chaperone who will introduce her to the right hostesses and of course get her accepted at Almack's."

"I have already arranged . . ." the Duke began.

"If you are thinking of the Governess, forget her," Gerald said. "What you want is someone of distinction who is respected by all the best hostesses. Surely there is one of your relations who can fit that bill?"

"I have actually been considering who could present her," the Duke said.

"You need someone to do a great deal more than that," Gerald answered, "and it must naturally be someone with an impeccable reputation."

The Duke knew quite well that Gerald was subtly warning him against Lady Isobel, and when he thought about it he knew she was one ⸱rson whom he had no wish for Alvina to meet.

⸱e had put her at the back of his mind while ⸱ in the country and had deliberately refrained from asking Gerald whether she was back in England.

Now, as if there was no need to ask the question, his friend said:

"Isobel arrived from Paris yesterday. She is staying at her father's house in Piccadilly and is expecting you to dine with her tonight."

"Why did you tell her I was back?" the Duke asked sharply.

"I did not have to tell her, she knew."

"How could she have known?"

"She sent a servant, I gather, to call here to enquire when you were expected, and since you did not tell your Butler to keep it a secret, he naturally gave the answer."

"Dammit!" the Duke said beneath his breath. "I really do not have time for Isobel at the moment."

"You will find that Isobel has very different ideas."

"She will be disappointed."

That, however, was easier said than done.

Before the Duke had time to send a note to her father's house to say he was unavoidably prevented from dining with her that evening, it was too late.

When he returned to Berkeley Square, having spent the afternoon visiting the Prince Regent and being enthusiastically received at Carlton House, he saw a carriage outside his house.

It was emblazoned with a very impressive coat-of-arms, and he knew that Isobel was waiting for him.

There was nothing he could do, because he was well aware that Isobel would continue to wait however long he remained away.

Bateson told him she had been in the house for over an hour, and he went into the Drawing-Room.

As the door closed behind him she rose from the chair in which she was sitting by the fireplace.

He had to admit she looked very lovely. She had discarded her thin cloak and also her bonnet, which was trimmed with a dozen small ostrich-feathers.

Her fashionable gown was almost transparent and revealed the perfection of her figure.

The Duke had only a glimpse of it before she ran down the room, her arms outstretched.

She threw herself against him and lifting her face to his looked up at him, her dark eyes filled with an expression of desire which he knew only too well.

Then, before he could even speak, her lips were on his.

She kissed him as he should have kissed her, passionately, demandingly, insistently.

As he felt her soft body press closer and closer to him, it was impossible for him not to put his arms round her.

It was only when she set him free that he managed to say:

"I did not expect you to arrive from France so soon."

"But you are glad I am here. Tell me, dearest,

that you are glad to see me!"

He was aware that the seductive note in Isobel's voice was somewhat contrived, but, at the same time, as her arms tightened round his neck he was aware that she was genuinely excited by his closeness and the kisses she had given him.

"Oh, Ivar," she went on before he could speak. "I have missed you. Paris was ghastly without you, despite the fact that the Prince de Conde paid me extravagant compliments and I had a dozen invitations for dinner every night."

With difficulty the Duke managed to extricate himself from her clinging arms, and walked towards the fireplace, saying as he did so:

"I am not surprised, Isobel. You are certainly in very good looks."

"Every man I meet tells me that," she said a little pettishly. "I want you to say that you have been dying without me."

"I am afraid that would not be true," the Duke replied, "for the simple reason that I have been busy."

"Too busy to think of me?"

Again she did not wait for him to answer, but said excitedly:

"Oh, Ivar, now that I am here, there are so many things for us to do together! Although I wanted to dine alone with you tonight, I think we will have to go to Carlton House."

The Duke smiled.

"I have just come from the Prince Regent and

he has made my attendance at dinner a Royal Command."

Isobel laughed.

"I thought he would do so. I dined with him last night and told him as a dead secret how much we mean to each other."

The Duke stiffened.

"I think that was a mistake."

"Why?" Isobel asked. "Everybody I have met has spoken to me of their delight that you are now the Duke, and of the wonders of your Castle."

She looked round the room and said:

"And this house is perfect for what we want in London. I have already seen the big *Salon* upstairs, and we can have at least one hundred and fifty people at our parties without it being a squeeze."

The Duke frowned.

"I can hardly believe that you inspected my house, Isobel, when I was not here to show it to you."

"Darling, do not be so stuffy!" she replied. "I wanted to be quite certain that we should be happy here, although of course we would be happy anywhere. At the same time, I must have the right background in order to play the perfect hostess."

The Duke was silent for a moment while he sought for words to inform Isobel that he had no intention of marrying anyone at the moment.

But the door opened and Gerald came in.

"I thought I should have to apologise for having kept you waiting," he said, "but Bateson tells me you have only just returned."

"That is true," the Duke replied.

Gerald crossed the room to raise Isobel's hands to his lips, saying:

"I thought I might find you here."

"I have been waiting for Ivar for over an hour," Isobel replied, "but as I have just said, I have not wasted my time."

"What have you been doing?" Gerald asked, as she obviously expected him to.

"I have been finding out that the house is perfect for us to entertain in, and I can see myself so clearly receiving our guests at the top of that very attractive staircase.

Gerald saw the Duke's lips tighten, and he said:

"You are taking your fences too fast, Isobel. I was informed only a few hours ago that as Ivar has much to do, he has no intention of marrying for years."

The Duke thought with an irrepressible smile that Gerald, ever since he became his friend, had always been prepared to come to his rescue in a tight corner.

"That is true," he agreed. "It will certainly be years before the Castle and the Estate are put to right and things are restored to what they were in the past."

There was silence, and Isobel looked from one man to the other.

"What is all this?" she asked.

Her voice now sounded a very different note, and she went on:

"Is this a conspiracy between you two?"

"Not in the least," Gerald replied, "but it is always wise, my dear Isobel, to face facts, and the fact is that Ivar, for the moment, is not in the marriage-market."

"That is nothing to do with you!" she said angrily. "I presume Ivar can speak for himself."

Then, as if she thought this attitude was unwise, she rose from the sofa, went to the Duke, and slipped her hand in his.

"We will talk about it when we are alone," she said very softly.

The Duke, as was expected of him, raised her hand to his lips.

"We will meet tonight at Carlton House."

"I am sure you will be kind enough to take me home afterwards," Isobel said in a child-like voice which she used when she was at her most dangerous. "Papa hates his horse and his coachmen being kept out late."

The Duke could not think of a reasonable way he could refuse, and she flashed a smile at Gerald but her eyes as she looked at him were hard as agates.

Then, as the Duke hurried to open the door for her, she moved down the room with a contrived grace which made her appear like a young goddess who had just stepped down from Olympus.

As she reached the Duke, she said in a voice that only he could hear:

"*Au revoir*, my love. I shall be counting the hours until tonight."

When he had seen her to her carriage at the front door, the Duke returned to where Gerald was waiting in the Drawing-Room.

"I suppose I ought to say 'thank you,' " he said. "I do not know whether you have made things worse or better."

"I do not think they could be much worse," Gerald replied, "unless you intend to marry Isobel."

The Duke did not answer, and he said:

"You know, Ivar, I never interfere in your love-affairs, but I think you ought to know that I learnt just now when I went to White's that the reason she left Paris so quickly was not only that she was following you."

The Duke waited, with a questioning look in his eyes, and Gerald went on:

"After you left, she behaved so outrageously with the *Duc* de Gramont that the *Duchesse* was furious, and there was a highly dramatic scene at a party, where I gather the whole of Paris was present, which made it imperative for Isobel to leave the next day."

The Duke walked across the room and back again before he said:

"I am glad you have told me. I am in a mess."

"I thought you would be," Gerald replied. "I told you she was determined to be a Duchess, and I cannot imagine a worse fate for any man

119

than to be married to Isobel."

The Duke knew this was true, but because Isobel had been so persistent, he had played with the idea of making her his wife.

Now he knew that he could never envisage her at the Castle, caring for his people who worked for him and worrying herself as to whether their children were educated or their grandparents had medical attention.

At the same time, he had the uncomfortable feeling that he was half-committed, and that Isobel, fastening onto him like a leech, would do everything in her power to prevent him getting away from her.

As if Gerald knew what he was thinking, he said:

"For God's sake, Ivar, be careful. She is a dangerous woman, and you will find it impossible to be free of her."

"No-one, not even Prinny, can make me marry someone I do not wish to marry!" the Duke said firmly.

"Do not be too sure of that," Gerald replied, "and the last thing you want at this particular moment is a scandal."

"That is true," the Duke agreed. "It is just another problem on top of the ones I am weighed down with already."

"I will give you something else to think about," Gerald said. "You may find it even more unpleasant."

"What is that?"

"Jason is calling on you tomorrow morning, and, from all I hear, you will either have to bail him out or let him go to the Fleet."

The Duke started.

The Fleet, which was the prison for debtors, was so notorious that any gentleman who was sent there for not being able to pay his debts received a great deal of publicity in the national newspapers.

He could not imagine anything which he would dislike more than for the world to know that his relative, and a Harling, was there.

At a moment when he was preparing to take his place in the House of Lords as the fifth Duke of Harlington, it would be impossible to admit that his cousin was incarcerated in the filth, vulgarity, and degradation of the debtors' prison.

Because it upset him even to think of it, the Duke's voice was harsh as he replied:

"I have already decided to see Jason and tell him that I will give him a fairly generous allowance, as long as he behaves himself."

"It will cost you a pretty penny to rescue him in the first place. I do not suppose he will thank you for it or agree to your conditions."

"I will make him agree!" the Duke said fiercely.

"How?" Gerald asked simply.

The Duke knew uncomfortably and unmistakably that he did not have the answer to that question.

Chapter Five

The Prince Regent retired early, with Lady Hertford on his arm.

One of the few things for which Lady Hertford was liked was that she did not wish to keep the Prince up late.

She was in fact getting on in years and was only too willing to end the evening far sooner than was hoped by those who surrounded the Prince Regent.

The Duke, watching them go, looked round for Gerald Chertson and saw him deep in conversation with Viscount Castlereagh, the Secretary of State for Foreign Affairs.

As he did not like to interrupt them unnecessarily, he walked slowly through the Reception-Rooms, noticing how many additions had been made since he was last in England.

The Prince's passion for collecting was one of the bits of gossip which had percolated through to the Armed Forces, besides rumours concerning his amatory affairs.

But, while the majority of the Duke's fellow-officers had strongly criticised the pile of debts accumulating from the treasures installed at Carlton House and the Royal Pavilion at Brighton, the Duke was sympathetic.

He was quite certain that future generations would acclaim the Prince Regent as a man of exceptionally good taste, but for the moment the only things that concerned the populace were his interest in women and the huge pile of unpaid debts.

Now the Duke stopped appreciatively before some Dutch paintings which the Prince Regent had bought early in the century, and thought how wise he had been to acquire them when they were inexpensive.

There were also some outstanding statues and a collection of miniatures which he appraised carefully, thinking with satisfaction that they were not as good as those he himself owned.

When he felt that Gerald must have finished his conversation, he saw him coming down the room towards him.

"Are you ready to leave?" Gerald asked.

"I am," the Duke replied, "but I did not like to interrupt you when I saw how seriously you were talking to Castlereagh."

"He was being extraordinarily interesting," Gerald said. "I will tell you about it as we drive home."

As they moved towards the door, he said as if it was an after-thought:

"By the way, I have not seen Isobel for some time."

"Neither have I," the Duke replied. "Do you suppose she has left?"

"It seems surprising that she should do so, unless she is annoyed with you."

The Duke thought this might be the reason.

He had ignored the invitation in Isobel's eyes when the gentlemen had joined the ladies after dinner and had deliberately talked to one of the other guests.

He had known without looking round that her eyes were dark with anger, and she had been tapping her fan irritably on the arm of her chair.

However, he had no intention of parading himself in public as a captive at Isobel's chariot-wheels, which he was sure she intended he should do.

Instead, he had gone out of his way the whole evening to avoid talking to her.

Therefore, he expected she was by now in one of her black moods, with which he had become familiar, and had probably found somebody else to take her home, being quite certain it would make him jealous.

There was certainly no sign of her amongst the other ladies who were collecting their wraps, and as he and Gerald settled themselves comfortably in the carriage that was waiting for them, Gerald said:

"You look pleased with yourself, Ivar, but I am quite certain Isobel will not let you off the hook so easily."

The Duke stiffened, and his friend knew that once again he was resenting the intrusion into his private affairs.

"I am sorry, Ivar," he said, "but because I am so fond of you, I want to make quite certain that your freedom, if nothing else, is not in danger."

The Duke did not reply, and after a moment Gerald went on:

"The night is still young. I suppose you would not like to do anything amusing? The Palace of Fortune has some extremely attractive new Cyprians whose praises were being sung in the Club this morning."

"To be honest," the Duke replied, "I have not only had quite a long day but I also have a lot to think about — in fact too much!"

Gerald laughed.

"You would soon be bored if you had nothing to do! All right, we will have an early night, but tomorrow I am taking you out on the town, whether you like it or not, otherwise you will find yourself growing old and staid beyond your years."

The Duke laughed.

"Now you are frightening me," he said, "but have it your own way. I shall need somebody to cheer me up after I have seen Jason tomorrow morning."

"That is underestimating the effect he will have

on you," Gerald answered.

The carriage drew up outside the house in Berkeley Square and the Duke alighted, telling the coachman to take Major Chertson to his lodgings in Half-Moon Street.

"I shall not need you anymore," he added.

The coachman saluted, touched his top-hat, and drove away.

The Duke walked through the front door, which he saw had been opened by one of the new footmen.

He was a young man who looked quite intelligent, and the Duke asked:

"What is your name?"

"Henry, Your Grace."

"And what were you doing before you came into my service?"

"I were in the Navy, Your Grace."

The Duke asked him what ship he had been in, and learnt that he was too young to have served for more than a year at sea, but on being discharged when the war was over he had found it difficult to obtain employment.

He told the Duke how grateful he was to be taken on at Harlington House and that he hoped he would give satisfaction.

The Duke, liking his bearing and the way in which he spoke, replied:

"I am sure you will, and remember to take notice of what Mr. Bateson tells you. He has been in service all his life, and there is nothing he does not know."

"I'll do me best, Your Grace."

The Duke smiled, and without going into any of the downstairs rooms started to climb the stairs to his bedroom.

When he reached the landing he looked back to see that Henry, having locked the front door, had installed himself comfortably in the round-topped padded armchair in which as night-footman he would spend the long hours until dawn.

Walking along the corridor, the Duke reached the Master Suite, which had been occupied by all the Dukes of Harlington.

Like his bedroom at the Castle, it was dominated by a huge, curtained four-poster bed which had been installed in the house in the reign of Queen Anne.

He entered the outer door into the small hallway in which a candle had been left burning in a silver sconce bearing the Harlington crest.

He saw there was a light in his bedroom, but when he pushed open the door he was surprised to find that his valet was not waiting for him.

The Duke told himself somewhat irritably that this was a slackness he could not countenance, and he walked across to the fireplace.

He had put out his hand towards the bell-pull when a soft voice from the bed said:

"I told your man I would wait up for you!"

The Duke started and turned round.

Lying in the great bed, half-hidden by the draped curtains, was Isobel.

She was wearing nothing but an emerald neck-lace which, even in his surprise at seeing her, the Duke realised was new.

It flashed through his mind that it might have been a gift from the *Duc* de Gramont.

Then in a slightly irritable tone he asked:

"What are you doing here, Isobel?"

"I am waiting for you, darling."

"I thought you had gone home."

It was a somewhat banal remark, but for the moment the Duke was finding it hard to think what he should do or how he should get rid of Isobel without creating a scene.

He realised she was being outrageous and be-having in a way which, if it ever became known, would cause a tremendous scandal.

He guessed, however, that this was what she intended, and he had walked into the trap she had set for him, from which it would be difficult to extricate himself.

As he stood looking at her, she held out her arms.

"I will explain to you everything you want to know," she said softly, "but it will be much easier to do so if you are closer."

Lying in the darkness, the Duke could hear Isobel's even breathing and knew she was fast asleep.

It was not surprising, as their love-making had been fiery and, from a physical point of view, very satisfying.

At the same time, he was aware that she had tempted him into a position from which it had been impossible to free himself without extremely unpleasant recriminations.

To save these, he had given her what she wanted.

The one candle which had been left alight in the room had flickered out, and now the only light came very faintly from the sides of the curtains so that the Duke thought there must be a moon in the sky.

Very softly, moving with the stealth that came from a perfectly controlled body and from the training he had instigated and insisted upon amongst his soldiers in Portugal, Spain, and France, he crept from the bed and crossed the carpet towards the door.

As he did so, he picked up from a chair the clothes he had been wearing, and still making no sound opened the door and passed outside.

His actions were as stealthy as any Tracker's, and as silent as those which he had taught his men were indispensable in making a surprise attack on the enemy in order to confuse and bewilder them.

In fact, the French had often been appalled to find, when they least expected it, that they were either surrounded or infiltrated by English soldiers whom they had neither heard nor seen approaching them.

Once outside the bedroom, the Duke moved into the room where he bathed and where his clothes were kept in large mahogany wardrobes.

He dressed himself swiftly, putting on the same silk stockings and knee-breeches he had worn at Carlton House, and his evening-coat with its long tails, on the breast of which were pinned a number of diamond-encrusted decorations.

He had managed, still without making any noise, to extract a fresh cravat from the drawer of the dressing-table, and he tied it swiftly with an expertise which always infuriated any valet who looked after him.

Then, looking exactly as he had done when he dined with the Prince Regent, he went from the Master Suite along the corridor and down the stairs into the Hall.

Henry was by this time asleep, and only when the Duke deliberately stepped noisily onto the marble floor did he awake with a start.

He jumped to his feet, and the Duke said:

"I have to go out again, Henry, and I expect I shall be late, but as soon as I have left I want you to run to the Duke of Melchester's stables at the back of Melchester House in Park Lane. Do you know where I mean?"

"I think so, Your Grace."

"Wake the coachman and tell him to come round here immediately to collect Lady Isobel Dalton and take her home."

"I'll do that, Your Grace."

"When the carriage arrives," the Duke went on, "fetch the head housemaid — I have forgotten her name — and ask her to help Lady

Isobel downstairs and into the carriage."

He thought the footman looked puzzled, and added:

"Explain to her that Lady Isobel is feeling ill and is therefore lying down until the carriage arrives. Do you understand?"

"I understands, Your Grace."

"Then do exactly as I have told you," the Duke said, "and try not to make any mistakes."

"I'll do my best, Your Grace."

"Good man!"

The Duke turned towards the door and Henry hastily unlocked it for him. Only as he stepped outside did the footman say, as if he had just thought of it:

"Your Grace don't want a carriage?"

"No, I am not going far," the Duke replied.

He walked away quickly, finding his way to Gerald Chertson's lodgings in Half-Moon Street, where the sleepy porter opened the door for him.

The Duke climbed a narrow flight of stairs to the second floor, where Gerald rented two small rooms for himself and one for his servant.

It took the Duke a little time to get any answer as he knocked on the flat door.

When finally it was opened by Gerald in his nightshirt his friend stared at him in astonishment.

"Ivar! What are you doing here at this hour?"

The Duke walked past him into the bedroom, where Gerald had lit one candle before responding to the insistent noise which had awakened him.

Briefly, in as few words as possible, the Duke explained what had happened.

"So that was why Isobel left early!" Gerald exclaimed. "We might have guessed she was up to some mischief!"

The Duke did not reply, and he said:

"You realise what this means, Ivar? She will tell her father tomorrow where she has been all night, and the Duke of Melchester will insist that you marry her."

"That is where you are mistaken," the Duke replied quietly. "I have sent my footman to Melchester House for her carriage to take her home, and have told him to wake my head housemaid and explain that Isobel has been taken ill and she is to help her into it."

Gerald stared at him.

"And you think she will go quietly?"

"There is nothing else she can do," the Duke replied.

"And where does that leave you?"

"It leaves me," the Duke answered, "with you at the most important party that is taking place in London tonight."

Gerald stared at him as if he had taken leave of his senses.

Then the Duke said:

"Come on, Gerald! You cannot be so stupid as not to realise that if I am seen dancing until dawn by everybody of any importance in the

Beau Monde, it will be impossible for Isobel to tell the world that we spent the night in each other's arms.

Gerald gave a sudden shout that seemed to vibrate round the small bedroom.

"Ivar, you are a genius!" he said. "God knows, I have seen you get out of some very tight spots, but never quite as subtly or cleverly as this!"

As he spoke, he jumped up from the bed on which he had been sitting and went to the mantelpiece, on which there was a stack of white cards engraved with the names of famous hostesses.

He picked up a handful of them and flung them down on the bed in front of the Duke.

"Pick out the best while I dress," he said.

The Duke lifted up the cards one by one, holding them so that the light from the candle fell on them.

There were six parties to which Major Gerald Chertson had been invited tonight, but by far the most important of them was the invitation sent by the Countess of Jersey.

The Countess had sprung into social fame when she captured the vacillating heart of the Prince of Wales and estranged him from Mrs. Fitzherbert, who was thought secretly to be his wife.

Marie Fitzherbert, much as she adored the Prince, had realised the truth of what Sheridan had said of him:

"He is too much of a Ladies' Man to be the man of any lady."

Although she was often exasperated by his self-ishness, she had always been ready to forgive him for his casual affairs in the past, but she had never been more jealous or miserable than when she realised he was falling in love with the Countess of Jersey.

The mother of two sons and seven daughters, some of whom had already provided her with grandchildren, the Countess was nine years older than the Prince, but she was a woman of immense charm and undeniable beauty.

In fact, at the time she was spoken of as having an "irresistible seductiveness and fascination."

The Prince's affair with the Countess had lasted for some years, and she had made the very most of the association by providing for herself a place in Society from which it would be impossible to tumble her.

The Duke knew now, using his instinct for self-preservation, that to have the Countess on his side would undoubtedly be a weapon that Isobel would find hard to match.

By the time Gerald Chertson, who like the Duke had dressed himself extremely quickly and without the help of his valet, returned to the room, his friend was waiting with the Countess's invitation-card in his hand.

"That is where we are going!" he said, holding it out.

"To hear is to obey!" Gerald replied mockingly, and they hurried down the stairs together.

"Have you come in your carriage?" Gerald

asked, as they reached the front door.

"No, we will have to take a hackney-cab," the Duke replied.

Fortunately, there was one just outside the house, crawling slowly down the street towards Piccadilly.

Gerald hailed it, and the two friends sat side by side as the cabby whipped up his tired horse.

"I am relying on you to introduce me," the Duke said. "I do not think I have seen the Countess for eight or nine years."

"She will welcome you with open arms," Gerald replied, "not only because she has never grown too old to appreciate a handsome man, but also because you are a Duke and she will be delighted to introduce you like a shy débutante to the *Beau Monde*."

"That is what I anticipated," the Duke said quietly.

Gerald threw back his head and laughed.

"I do not believe this is happening!" he said. "It is so like you, Ivar! I have never known you without a crisis in your life, or some incredible surprise which nobody could have anticipated."

He laughed again as he said:

"I thought we were going to have a quiet night. I only wish I could see Isobel's face when your housemaid wakes her to say that her father's carriage is waiting outside to take her home!"

"I would rather not think of it."

"Mark my words, she will not give up," Gerald continued. "She will merely dig in her spurs and be more determined than ever to wear the Harlington coronet."

"Then she will be disappointed!" the Duke said grimly.

When they reached the Earl of Jersey's house it was not yet two o'clock and the Ball-Room was still crowded.

The Countess, looking resplendent and still, despite her age, an attractive woman, held out her hands with delight as Gerald Chertson approached her.

"So you have arrived," she exclaimed, "when I had despaired, you naughty boy, of seeing you!"

Gerald kissed her hand.

"You must forgive me for being late," he said, "but I have been showing my friend Ivar Harling, who has only just arrived back in London, some of the amusements he has been missing while he has been in France."

The Countess held out her hand to the Duke with what was obviously a sincere gesture of pleasure.

"I had no idea that you were in England," she said, "or I would already have sent you a dozen invitations!"

"You are the first person, with the exception of His Royal Highness, whom I have visited," the Duke said truthfully.

The Countess was delighted.

In the space of a few minutes she introduced him to a dozen people, giving them, as she did so, a potted biography of his achievements.

She made the Duke aware that while he had been abroad and out of sight, she had not been ignorant of his new importance in the Social World.

By the time he had talked to a number of people and had even danced twice round the room with his hostess, the Duke was delighted by the suggestion that they should repair to the Supper-Room.

There, at a table precided over by the Countess, he found the conversation witty and slanderous and as stimulating as the excellent champagne.

It was long after dawn when he and Gerald left, and by that time the Duke had managed to take the Countess on one side.

"I believe that only you can help me," he said simply.

"In what way?" the Countess questioned.

He was aware of the look of curiosity in her eyes.

He told her briefly of his predecessor's illness, and how he had not only expected his daughter to take care of him but had also prevented her from seeing her relations or friends and had convinced her that they were penniless.

The Duke did not go into details about what had happened on the Estate but was concerned only to evoke the Countess's sympathy for Alvina.

He told her how she had been unable to spend a penny on herself or enjoy any of the social activities that should have been hers when she had left the School-Room.

"What am I to do about her?" the Duke asked when the story was finished.

"I can see it is a problem," the Countess replied, "but certainly not an insoluble one. I imagine, as head of the family, you will now provide for her?"

"Of course!" the Duke confirmed. "But she needs a Chaperone to introduce her to Society, and somebody who could take her to the best dressmakers."

The Countess smiled.

"There should be no difficulty about that," she said. "What woman could resist the idea of ordering a whole wardrobe of new clothes, even if they are for somebody else?"

"Then you will help me find the right person?"

"Send her to stay with me first," the Countess said, "and when I have dressed her, as you suggest, and made the first introductions, I will find somebody eminently suitable to carry on the good work."

"I cannot thank you enough," the Duke exclaimed. "At the same time, I do not like to impose on your good nature."

"I shall expect my reward."

"What is that?" he asked.

"That you will come to parties and let me find you a wife who will grace the end of your table and the Harlington diamonds."

The Duke laughed.

"Could any woman, even including Your Ladyship, refrain from match-making?"

His voice was more serious as he went on:

"I will do anything you ask, except allow you to hurry me up the aisle before I have had a holiday, and a long one! Wellington has been a hard taskmaster these last years, and I am afraid a wife might be an even more exacting one."

"I will find you somebody soft, sweet, gentle, and very amenable," the Countess promised.

"I doubt if such a paragon exists," the Duke replied, "but in the meantime let me enjoy myself as a bachelor. I feel I deserve it."

The Countess glanced at the decorations on his breast.

"I suppose you do," she admitted. "At the same time, my dear boy, you are far too attractive and far too handsome not to have every woman in London endeavouring to get you into her clutches!"

The Duke remembered that that was exactly what Isobel was trying to do, and he said:

"It sounds very enjoyable after being a target for French marksmen for more years than I care to remember."

"Now you are far more likely to die of kisses," the Countess promised. "And here is somebody I particularly want you to meet."

As she spoke she beckoned to a very attractive Beauty who had just come into the Supper-Room.

She came obediently towards her hostess, who

introduced the Duke and insisted that they should have the last dance together.

By the end of it the Duke knew he had made a new conquest, and he had promised to call on his new acquaintance the following afternoon.

"I shall be waiting for Your Grace," she said very softly as they said good-night.

The Duke and Gerald left together, and as by now the sun was golden in the East and the last stars were receding in the sky, they decided to walk home.

"I feel I need some fresh air," the Duke said.

"I thought you were behaving admirably," Gerald said approvingly. "Our hostess was wildly enthusiastic about you, and she also told me she has promised to take your cousin under her wing. That was a clever move on your part."

"I thought that myself," the Duke agreed. "Alvina will certainly get off on the right foot."

"The Countess, if I know anything of her methods, will have her married and off your hands in a few months."

The Duke did not respond, and Gerald looked at him enquiringly, then realised he was frowning.

"There is no need for such haste," he said.

As he spoke, he wondered why the idea of marriage for Alvina as well as for himself made him feel angry.

He had set the wheels in motion, but now that they were actually turning, he thought perhaps he had been too impetuous.

It might have been better if he had left things as they were, at least for a little while longer.

The Duke awoke and realised it was later than he had intended.

At the same time, his valet, having learnt that he had come to bed after dawn had broken, had left him to sleep.

When he had reached his bedroom it was to find that everything had been tidied, and it was difficult to believe that when he had come home earlier Isobel had been lying against his pillows wearing nothing but an emerald necklace.

As he undressed and got back into bed, he could not help thinking with a smile how shocked many of his ancestors would have been at her behaviour and, if it came to that, at his.

Somehow he had saved himself, although now, when he thought of it, he realised it had been a very "close shave."

It had been clever of Isobel to think out a situation in which it would have been impossible for him to do anything but offer her marriage.

The Duke of Melchester was a highly respected member of the aristocracy and a gentleman of the "Old School."

He would certainly have demanded that his daughter's honour be protected, and there would have been no way of refusing to obey what the whole Social World would have thought of as a dictate of honour.

"I am free!" the Duke said to himself as he closed his eyes.

Then, almost as if there were a little devil sitting on his shoulder, a voice asked:

"But for how long?"

As Gerald had warned the Duke, the interview at eleven o'clock the next morning with his cousin Jason was extremely unpleasant.

Jason arrived looking, in the Duke's eyes, over-dressed.

If there was one thing he and the Duke of Wellington disliked, it was the "Dandies" who affected ridiculously high cravats, over-square shoulders, over-tight waists, and pantaloons which had to be dampened before they could pull them up over their hips.

The points of Jason's collar were high over his chin, and his cravat made it appear as if it was difficult for him to breathe. The shoulders of his coat were too square, and the sleeves bulged high above them, making them appear in the Duke's eyes almost grotesque.

He carried a lace-edged handkerchief which was saturated with perfume and which he held delicately to his nose.

At the same time, the Duke was aware that his eyes were hard, shrewd, and avaricious.

Jason was five years older than his cousin, and the Duke thought he was increasingly anxious to ensure that his future should be a comfortable one and that he should be very much better off financially than he had been in the past.

He wondered, as he had wondered before, why Jason had not found a rich wife.

But he was sure no decent woman would marry him, and Jason was too snobby and too proud of his Harling blood to consider marriage with some wealthy tradesman's daughter, who might have been prepared to accept him.

He had therefore relied on borrowing from his friends, and gambling, but he often ran up debts which, as at the moment, he had no possible chance of paying without the help of the family.

The Duke knew when they met in the Library that Jason was wondering how much he could extract from him by blackmailing him with the fear of scandal and adverse publicity.

Somewhat coldly he offered Jason a drink, which he accepted.

Then the cousins sat down, eying each other like two bull-dogs, the Duke thought, each waiting for the other to attack.

The Duke took the initiative.

"I am quite aware, Jason, of why you wished to see me," he said. "I have already been told that you are in debt, and I think it would be best if you were frank and told me exactly what is the sum involved."

His cousin named a figure which made the Duke want to gasp, but with his usual self-control his face remained impassive.

"Is that everything?" he asked.

"Everything I can think of," Jason replied surlily.

There was a short silence. Then, as if he found it intolerable, Jason went on:

"It is all very well for you, Ivar, to walk into a fortune without having to lift a finger for it, but surely you will admit it is the most astounding good luck, and as head of the family you should help those who were not born under the same lucky star."

His last sentence was spoken in a sneering tone that was unmistakable, and the Duke said quietly:

"I admit I have been very fortunate. I am therefore, Jason, prepared to do two things."

"What are they?"

"The first is to pay your present outstanding bills," the Duke replied, "the second, to grant you in the future an allowance of a thousand pounds a year."

Jason Harling's eyes lit up on hearing that the Duke would settle his bills for him, but even so he said quickly:

"Two thousand!"

"One thousand!" the Duke replied coldly. "And there is of course a condition attached."

"What is it?"

Now there was no mistaking that Jason's expression was hostile.

"You go abroad and do not come back to England for at least five years."

Jason stared at him incredulously.

"Do you mean that?"

"I mean it!" the Duke said firmly. "If you do not agree, the whole deal is off."

Jason jumped to his feet.

"I do not believe it!"

"Then you can settle your debts yourself, and I shall not lift a finger to help you!"

"I have never heard of anything so diabolical!" Jason shouted furiously.

"I think, actually, that I am being extremely generous," the Duke said. "The debts you have run up are so enormous that it would not surprise me in the slightest if you end up in the Fleet. But, as there are a great number of other calls on the family purse, it is essential that this sort of situation should not arise again."

"In other words, you want to spend it all on yourself!" Jason said spitefully.

"That is quite untrue, and I have no intention of arguing," the Duke replied. "But when you visited the Castle the other day you must have been aware that an enormous amount of money needs to be spent on the Estate: the Schools must be opened, and the Orphanages repaired or rebuilt."

He paused to say more slowly:

"More important than anything else, the tenant-farmers need funds to bring their farms back to the standard that existed ten years ago."

As he spoke, the Duke realised that all this meant nothing to Jason and he was thinking only of himself.

"I have no wish to live abroad," he said like a sulky child.

"I am sure you will find yourself very much at home in Paris or any other town in France," the Duke replied, "and quite frankly, Jason, I want you out of the country and out of people's sight when our cousin Alvina makes her début."

"I am not in the least concerned with Cousin Alvina," Jason answered, "but with my own life, and I wish to live in England."

"Then I hope you will find ways of doing so," the Duke said, rising to his feet.

Jason, looking up at him, realised that he was up against a brick wall.

There was a long silence before he said furiously:

"Damn you! I have no alternative but to do as you insist, have I?"

"I am afraid not," the Duke agreed.

"Very well!"

Jason rose and drew from the tail of his coat a sheath of bills.

"Here you are!" he said, slapping them down on a table. "The sooner they are met, the better, otherwise you will undoubtedly have the indignity of bailing me out of a locked cell!"

The Duke thought it would be far better if he was left in one, but he said quickly:

"I will pay the first part of your allowance into the branch of Coutt's Bank in Paris, unless you prefer some other major city. I shall also make it clear that you cannot draw from that account unless you present the cheque in person."

Jason did not reply, but as he stood in front of him the Duke saw that his fingers were clenched as if he would have liked to hit him.

Instead, he said in a voice that was fraught with venom:

"Very well, Cousin Ivar, you win for the moment! But never forget that the victor today is often the loser tomorrow!"

He walked towards the door, and as he reached it he looked back and the Duke thought he had never seen hatred so vehement in any man's eyes or in the expression on his face.

Then, as if words failed him, Jason walked out of the Library and the Duke heard his footsteps going down the corridor towards the Hall.

Chapter Six

Arriving back at the Castle after riding, Alvina was humming happily to herself.

It was so exciting to be in a position to engage servants for the house and men to work in the gardens, and to be able to assure the pensioners that their cottages would be repaired and their pensions increased.

Already, because news flew on wings, the villagers were aware of what was happening, and the excitement was spreading all over the two thousand acres the Duke owned round the Castle.

Alvina was quite certain that those on the Duke's other properties also had already learnt that things were changing, and that servants in every department who had been discharged after years of service were being re-employed.

"It is all so wonderful!" Alvina said to herself.

She thought the years when her father had declared over and over again that they had no money were like a nightmare from which she had at last awakened.

The Duke had been gone for five days, but time seemed to fly past and Alvina had not felt lonely.

In fact, she had so many people to see, so much to talk about, and so much to do that she was hardly aware of being alone as she had been in the past.

At the same time, although he was not there, the Duke seemed to be with her.

It was impossible not to think of him all the time and be aware that it was due to him alone that everything was changed.

If she had wanted more positive proof of his kindness, she had received it this morning when, after she had breakfasted with a choice of three dishes, which was a new experience, a Post-Chaise had arrived from London.

For a moment she thought excitedly that the Duke had returned.

But instead several large boxes were handed to one of the new footmen, who was learning his duties under Walton.

"These are for you, M'Lady," the young man said as Alvina came into the Hall, unable to restrain her curiosity as to what was happening.

"For me?" she exclaimed.

Then as she saw the name printed on one of the boxes, she had an idea what they contained.

The footman carried them up to her bedroom.

When she opened them, with the help of old Emma, who seemed to take on a new lease of life since she had help, Alvina saw that they were gowns which she had never dreamt she would have the chance of owning.

There were four of them, two for the day, two for the evening, and a third box contained a smart, thin summer riding-habit that seemed to her to have stepped straight out of a Fashion-Plate.

Almost before she had time to look at them, Alvina was joined by three of the new house-maids, who all came from the village, together with Mrs. Johnson, Mrs. Walton, and even two of the kitchen-maids.

She knew they were acting unconventionally, but she understood that because they shared with her the bad times, they now wished to share the good.

She held up the gowns for their inspection, one after another, and because she was so excited she put on the habit so that they could see her in it.

"It's just how you should look, M'Lady!" Mrs. Walton exclaimed. "Now we know the old days are back and we can all be happy again."

The way she spoke was so moving that Alvina felt the tears come into her eyes.

Impulsively she bent and kissed Mrs. Walton, saying:

"Whatever good times come to me, I intend to share them with you. You have been so wonderful these last years."

She nearly added: "when Papa was mad," but thought it would sound disloyal.

She felt anyway they were thinking the same thing and were aware that her father's mind had become deranged after Richard's death.

Yesterday two horses had arrived from London, which had been a thrill that was almost as exciting as her new gowns.

She knew instinctively that one of them had been chosen for her and was exactly the sort of horse that any Lady would wish to ride.

The other was a huge stallion, and she thought that the Duke would look magnificent on him and wanted him to come home so that they could ride together.

When she had gone to bed last night she had told herself that there would be so many things for him to do in London, so many people ready to welcome him, that she must wait patiently for his reappearance and not be surprised if he was a long time in coming.

Because she had lived such a quiet life, she knew very little about men, but she was not so stupid as not to realise how handsome the Duke was and that he had a presence that would make him stand out in any company, however distinguished.

'Perhaps,' she thought, 'he will find life in London, when he has Harlington House re-staffed, more attractive than living here.'

She was aware that it would take a little time before people in the County realised that the

Duke would be willing to receive them as her father had refused to do.

Therefore, he might discover that London was more congenial and certainly more amusing.

She found herself wondering what he would talk about to the beautiful women whom she was sure he would meet at Carlton House, and who would welcome him into the most distinguished and at the same time most sophisticated society in Europe.

She knew very little about the Social World of London except what she had read in the Court Columns of the newspapers or heard discussed in the village.

Strangely enough, that had been quite a mine of information.

Several of the sons and daughters of the villagers had originally gone to London to work at Harlington House.

When on her father's instructions they had been dismissed, they had fortunately obtained employment in the houses of other distinguished aristocrats.

This meant that their parents were kept informed of what was happening in London, and every letter and every piece of news which came by post or carrier was repeated round the village the moment it arrived.

Alvina therefore was well aware of the dislike the populace had for Lady Hertford because she was the latest fancy of the Prince Regent.

She had also heard over the years of the love-affairs of Lord Byron and a number of other noblemen, many of which were positively scandalous.

Although she told herself she should not listen, and certainly should not talk familiarly with people who were not of the same station as herself, she had nobody else to talk to.

It would have been unnatural for her to refuse to listen to what Mrs. Walton's niece wrote home about what she called the "goings-on of the smart young gentleman" in whose parents' house she was at present employed.

At the time, it had merely amused her, and she had forgotten what she heard almost as soon as it was spoken.

Now she began to imagine the Duke at parties, Balls, and Assemblies, surrounded by beautiful women and finding them very alluring after the long years of war.

'Perhaps he will never come back to the Castle,' she thought dismally.

Then she told herself there was no need for such depressing thoughts.

That he had thought of her in sending her such beautiful clothes raised her hopes that she would see him soon.

Last night she had sat up late making a list of all the people in the County whom he might invite to the Ball he was planning.

She also worked hard in supervising the new housemaids and the footmen as they cleaned the Ball-Room.

It was a tremendous task to wash down the walls, but when it was done the paint looked white and clear, and the gold-leaf which ornamented the cornice shone as brightly as it had when it was first applied.

The paintings on the walls were also improved by being dusted and having the dust scrubbed from their gold frames.

However, Alvina discovered it was going to take a long time to get the polish back on the floor.

The footmen not only got down on their knees to rub the polish in, but on Alvina's instructions tied dusters over their shoes and slid up and down until the parquet began to look very much brighter than it had for twenty years.

"The Duke when he gets back will be pleased with what I have done," Alvina told herself.

As she reached the top of the steps she turned back to watch the groom taking away the horse she had ridden that morning, and felt with a little lilt of her heart that she was sure the Duke had chosen it especially for her.

She walked into the Hall and smiled at the two footmen on duty, their newly polished crested buttons gleaming in the sunshine.

"Enjoy your ride, M'Lady?" one of them asked.

"Yes, thank you," Alvina replied.

She walked up the staircase, wondering as she did so if the Duke realised that a new stair-carpet was needed and thinking it should be one of the things to suggest to him when he returned.

She reached the top of the stairs and was just turning towards her bedroom when she saw to her surprise that at the far end of the corridor there was a man.

He was just outside the Master Suite, and for one moment she thought it was the Duke who had returned without her being aware of it.

Then she saw that it was not he, and it was also not a servant.

Feeling curious, she walked towards the man, wondering who he could be and why the footmen had not told her there was somebody strange in the house.

The corridor was long, and in that part of the building even in the daytime there was very little light.

Yet, before she had gone very far, Alvina was aware who her visitor was.

There was no mistaking the exaggerated square shoulders of what she knew was called a "Tulip of Fashion," and the high, elaborate cravat which made its owner carry his head at an almost imperious angle.

She was halfway towards the intruder, who, looking at the paintings to the right and the left of him, was not aware of her until they were within speaking distance.

Then Alvina ejaculated:

"Cousin Jason! Nobody told me you were here!"

"I saw you riding across the Park," Jason

Harling replied, "and I saw no reason to disturb your ride."

"I was not aware that you were calling," Alvina answered, "otherwise I would have been at home to welcome you."

"There is no need for us to stand on ceremony with each other," Jason Harling replied, "and as a Harling I look on the Castle as home, as of course you do."

The way he spoke made Alvina aware that he was being subtly offensive, although nothing he said in words was actually rude.

"Now that I am back," Alvina said, making an effort to speak pleasantly, "I hope I can offer you a cup of tea, or perhaps some other refreshment?"

"How kind of you!" Jason replied.

She was sure he was being sarcastic, but she turned to walk back towards the staircase.

As she did so, she wondered if she should ask Jason what he was doing wandering about the house and if he had been in the Master Suite.

She instinctively knew that he had, but she did not know quite how to put her suspicions into words.

They walked down the staircase in silence, and when they reached the Hall she said:

"Which would you prefer, Cousin Jason? Tea? Or perhaps a glass of wine . . . ?"

Before she could finish speaking, she saw that Walton was there, and Jason, without waiting for her to give the order, said to him:

"Bring a bottle of champagne to the Library!"

He spoke sharply and authoritatively, and as Alvina looked at him in surprise, so did Walton.

Then the Butler answered quietly:

"Very good, Mr. Jason, and would you require anything to eat?"

"No, just champagne," Jason replied, and walked towards the Library door.

Because she was determined not to show how astonished she was at his behaviour, Alvina said:

"The Drawing-Room is open, if you prefer."

"I am quite happy in here," Jason said, as a footman opened the Library door for them. "I suppose you are aware that every Museum in Europe would pay a fortune for the Shakespeare Folio, and the first edition *we* own of the *Canterbury Tales*?"

He accentuated the word "we" in a manner that was impossible for Alvina to ignore, and she said quietly:

"I think you are well aware, Cousin Jason, that the contents of the Castle belong to the reigning Duke only for his lifetime."

"Of course I am aware of that," Jason replied, "but it depends upon how long he reigns."

As he spoke, Alvina had an impression of evil that almost made her wince away from Jason Harling.

It was so vivid that for a moment she thought she was imagining it just because she disliked him.

Then, as she saw the expression in his eyes, she

felt she must recoil as if he were a reptile waiting to strike at her.

With what was an obvious effort to control what he was feeling, Jason flung himself down in one of the armchairs in front of the fireplace.

"Well, Cousin Alvina," he said, in a different tone of voice, "you have certainly fallen on your feet, and let me congratulate you on your riding-habit. It is certainly an improvement on what you were wearing when I last came here!"

Because Alvina was aware that he was being deliberately unpleasant, she merely inclined her head, and Jason went on:

"Rooms open, horses in the stable, footmen in the Hall! The new Duke is certainly flinging his money about in a profligate fashion."

There was a pause before he continued:

"Actually, I have come here to say good-bye to you, and of course to the Castle, the family seat of the Harlings, of which I am one."

"Good-bye?" Alvina questioned.

"Has the reigning Duke, my inestimable cousin, the gallant General of a hundred campaigns, not told you of what he has planned for me?"

He was speaking now in a jeering, mocking voice that seemed to jar the very air round them, and after a moment Alvina faltered:

"Cousin Ivar has . . . not yet returned from . . . London."

"Of course not!" Jason said. "He is enjoying himself as the new 'Lion' of the Season, the pet of the Countess of Jersey, and undoubtedly a very ardent lover of the most acclaimed Beauty of the Season."

Alvina sat upright and, clasping her fingers together because she was agitated, said in a carefully controlled tone:

"I do not think, Cousin Jason, that you should speak to me like that!"

"Have I shocked you?" he asked. "Oh, well, you will have to get used to shocks where our dashing cousin is concerned. He has deserted Lady Isobel, who declares that he promised her marriage, and if her father does not call him out, then doubtless the husband of his present inamorata will not be so cowardly."

Alvina rose to her feet.

"I have no wish to listen to you saying such things, and I think, Cousin Jason, that when you have finished your glass of wine you should be on your way."

Jason laughed and it was not a pleasant sound.

"Turning me out, are you? And by what right?"

Fortunately, before Alvina could answer, the door opened and Walton came in, followed by a footman carrying a silver tray on which there was a bottle of champagne in an ice-cooler.

He set it down on the grog-table which stood in a corner of the Library, and after a glass of champagne had been poured for Jason and Alvina had refused one, the servants withdrew.

Because she thought it degrading to quarrel while the servants were in the room, Alvina said nothing until the door shut. Then she said:

"You said just now that you had come here to say good-bye. Does that mean you are leaving England?"

"So you do know!" Jason said accusingly.

"Know what?" Alvina asked in bewilderment.

"That our cousin, the new Duke, has exiled me from my own country, my friends, and my family."

He made a sound of sheer disgust.

"Oh, yes, Cousin Alvina, you may look surprised, but that is what he has done — turned me out, lock, stock, and barrel. Unless I do what he says, he will have me thrown into prison and leave me to rot there rather than raise a finger to save me from such a fate."

"I do not believe it!" Alvina exclaimed.

"It is true! You can ask him when you see him. In the meantime, make no mistake, I shall have my revenge, and it will not be a pleasant one!"

"I do not know what you are talking about."

Jason emptied his glass and walked across the room to fill it again up to the brim from the bottle in the ice-cooler.

"There have been Harlings all through history who have survived the vengeance of Kings and the enemies with whom they have come in contact," he said. "But make no mistake, Ivar Harling will not survive the curse I have put upon him — the Curse of the Harlings, which will ensure that he dies slowly and in agony."

Alvina gave a little cry.

"Do not . . . talk like . . . that! How can you say
. . . such wicked things?"

"I say them because I know they will come
true," Jason said slowly.

He lifted his glass and added in a voice that
seemed to ring round the Library:

"To the future, and to the moment when we
hear the Duke is dead! Long live the Duke!"

As he spoke he tipped the whole glass of champagne down his throat, and without another
word went from the Library, leaving Alvina
staring after him in sheer astonishment.

Because of the way he had spoken, and because he seemed to leave an atmosphere of evil
behind him, she found it hard to move.

In fact, it was hard to do anything but feel that
she had come in contact with something that was
so wicked and beastly that she felt contaminated
by it.

Then at last she told herself that Jason was
mad, as mad as her father had been, and she
would not be afraid or over-awed by him.

She walked towards the door, but even as she
reached the Hall she heard the sound of wheels
outside and knew that Jason was driving away.

By the time she could see him from the front
door, he was crossing the bridge over the lake in
a smart, lightly sprung Phaeton with huge
wheels, drawn by a team of four horses which he
was driving at a tremendous pace.

As he went up the drive, the dust billowed out
behind him, and Alvina had the uncomfortable

thought that he was driving a chariot of fire.

"How can he hate Cousin Ivar?" she asked herself.

Then she was afraid of the answer.

Two hours later, when Alvina had changed from her riding-habit and was arranging some flowers in the Drawing-Room, she heard voices in the Hall.

She had time only to put down the flowers she held in her arms and turn to the door as it opened and the Duke came in.

At the sight of him Alvina gave a little cry and without thinking ran towards him eagerly.

"You are back!" she exclaimed. "How wonderful! I have been . . . longing for your . . . return."

"If I have been a long time you must forgive me," the Duke said in his deep voice, "but I had a great deal to do in London."

"I was sure of that," Alvina replied, "but there is so much for you to see here, and your horses have arrived."

"I thought they would please you," he said. "There are several more arriving tomorrow, and I hope some others next week."

Alvina clasped her hands together.

"We have been working desperately hard in repairing the stables," she said. "I know you will be pleased . . . and I want to show you the Ball-Room . . . and the carpenters and painters have . . . started work on the pensioners' cottages."

She spoke quickly and breathlessly, having been waiting for this moment to tell him of all the things she had been doing.

Then, as if she suddenly remembered that the Duke had travelled all the way from London, she said apologetically:

"But you must be thirsty, and I am sure Walton will be bringing you something to drink."

As she spoke, Walton came in with a footman carrying a tray just as he had done a few hours earlier.

Alvina realised with a little throb of fear as she thought of it, that she would have to tell the Duke that Jason had been to the Castle.

'I will tell him later,' she thought, wanting to postpone for as long as possible something that was unpleasant.

Only when the Duke was sipping his glass of champagne did she realise that he was looking at her searchingly and with what she thought was a twinkle in his eyes.

"I suppose first," she said a little shyly, "I should have thanked you for the . . . wonderful gowns you sent me. I can hardly believe they are . . . really mine! In fact, I do not feel myself, but somebody quite different!"

"You look very lovely in what you are wearing now," the Duke said.

He paid her the compliment in his usual calm, rather dry voice, so that it did not make Alvina feel shy, and she only asked:

"How can you have been so clever as to know

163

exactly the sort of gowns I would want to wear?"

"I cannot take all the credit," the Duke confessed. "They were in fact chosen for you by one of the most important women in the Social World, who has most graciously promised to present you to Society and ensure that from the moment you arrive in London you will be a great success."

The Duke spoke with a note of satisfaction in his voice and as he did so did not realise that Alvina stiffened.

"Whom . . . are you talking . . . about?" she asked, and her voice seemed to tremble.

"I am referring to the Countess of Jersey," the Duke replied. "You may not have heard of her, but she is a leader of London Society, and I can think of nobody who would be a more advantageous Chaperone to introduce you to all the people you should know."

There was silence. Then Alvina said in a very small voice:

"I . . . I thought . . . the Countess of Jersey was . . . at one time a very . . . close friend of the Prince Regent."

The Duke raised his eye-brows.

He had somehow thought that Alvina, living so quietly in the country, would not have been aware of the scandal and gossip there had been about the Countess.

However, it had all ended a long time ago, and he knew that it certainly would not affect now the reputation of any girl to whom she extended her patronage.

At the same time, he was suddenly aware of how innocent and unsophisticated Alvina was.

It struck him that perhaps it would be a mistake to plunge her into the very centre of a social vortex with its intrigues, its liaisons, and inevitably its promiscuous women like Isobel and the lovely creature with whom he had dined last night.

Because he had not before considered this aspect in regard to Alvina, he walked to the window to stand staring out into the garden.

He was wondering if he had made a mistake and questioning the arrangements he had made.

It occurred to him that if she was not shocked by what she found in the Social World, contact with it might spoil her.

He was so used to the women with whom he associated taking for granted the love-affairs which filled their lives, and believing that fidelity to their husbands was out-of-date, that he had not thought of Alvina as being completely different.

Now he realised he was dealing with a very young, unspoilt, unworldly girl, and he knew that the Countess of Jersey's involvement with the Prince had genuinely shocked her.

After a moment, when he knew Alvina was waiting for him to speak and was looking at him enquiringly, he said:

"I thought when I made the arrangement with

the Countess that I was doing what was best for you, since she is undoubtedly the Leader of the Social World as we know it."

"I . . . I have been thinking over your suggestion that . . . I should go to London," Alvina said, "and I would not want you to think me . . . ungrateful . . . but if it is possible . . . I would much rather . . . stay here."

She spoke hesitatingly, and after a moment the Duke said:

"I think it would be best for you to extend your horizons."

"I understand what you are saying to me," Alvina replied, "and I know how . . . ignorant and how foolish you must . . . think me . . . but it would be different if . . . Mama were with me . . . or even if I had a father on whom I could rely for guidance and . . . to prevent me from making mistakes."

She made a little gesture with her hands which was somehow pathetic.

As she spoke, the Duke thought of the conversation that had taken place at the Countess of Jersey's dinner-party.

He remembered that although it had been sophisticated, witty, and undoubtedly amusing, there had been a *double entendre* in every other word, and he now thought that a great deal had been said which was very unsuitable for a young girl to listen to.

Almost as if he could see a picture unroll in front of him, he could see the expression in Lady

Isobel's eyes when she looked at him, and that look duplicated in the eyes of a dozen other women with whom he had danced, talked, and dined.

It was something with which he had grown very familiar in Paris, and he had almost taken it for granted.

Women were all the same, and they wanted only one thing from him.

But now he was aware that Alvina was very different.

He had not missed the lilt in her voice when he came into the room and the expression of joy and happiness in her eyes because he was back.

He suddenly felt that she was part of the sunshine outside, the flowers in the garden, the freshness of the air, and the birds that flew above the trees.

She was youth, she was spring. She was as clear as the sky overhead and the water silver in the lake.

Feeling almost that he was being accused of trying to commit a crime, he said as if to defend himself:

"I thought I was arranging what was best for you!"

"You are so kind, so very, very kind," Alvina said, "and you know I will do anything you really want me to . . . but please, this is where I belong . . . and there is nothing in London which could be more wonderful than being here in this . . . lovely Castle."

There was a little tremor in her voice as she spoke, as if it was already being taken away from her, and the Duke said:

"Shall we talk about it later? I want to look at all the improvements you have been making, and of course to see the Ball-Room."

At his words she made a little sound of excitement, and quite unself-consciously she put her hand into his as she said:

"Come and look at the Ball-Room. I know it is going to surprise you, and everybody has worked so very, very hard so that you would be pleased."

The Duke's fingers closed over hers, and as they did so he told himself that he had to think about what he should do with her all over again.

One thing was more important than anything else — she must not be spoilt.

Dinner was over, and Alvina was wearing one of her new gowns, in which she felt like the Princess in a fairy-story.

It was white gauze, and in the new fashion was elaborately trimmed with frills and flowers round the hem.

There were also flowers on the small puffed sleeves which revealed her shoulders, the whiteness of her skin, and her long swan-like neck.

The Duke had looked at her critically as she joined him in the Drawing-Room before dinner and knew she could hold her own in any London Ball-Room.

She would undoubtedly be acclaimed as a Beauty as soon as she appeared.

There was something about her that was very distinctive and, he thought, unusual.

After scrutinising her with a connoisseur's eye, he decided that she looked different from other women he had known because there was something untouched, perhaps spiritual, about her that had been missing in all of them.

He could not exactly describe it, except that he knew it was part of the same feeling he had had about the Castle when he was young.

If he had thought of himself, as he had, as a Knight, and the Castle itself had been peopled with Knights, then Alvina fitted in as one of their Ladies, filled with the same ideals of chivalry and honour.

That was what motivated the Knights, and if they were prepared to wage war against what was wrong and evil, so in their own way the women to whom they returned with the spoils of victory had the same standards from which they never faltered.

As they talked at dinner and the candles on the table illuminated Alvina's face, the Duke thought her beauty had a subtlety that grew on the mind and on the imagination.

It was very different from a loveliness that was entirely physical.

He had grown used to knowing that every woman he met since hostilities had ceased had only one object, which was to arouse him physically into admiring and desiring her.

He knew when he considered it that while Alvina looked upon him with admiration, listened to him appreciatively, and was obviously thrilled to be with him, her feelings for him were very different.

She had no idea how to flirt, no idea how to turn the conversation so as to make it personal to her, whatever subject they might be discussing.

She did not attempt to touch him with intimate little gestures that were meant to be provocative.

Her lips did not curve to entice him, nor was there an invitation in her eyes.

Instead, she had an aura of happiness about her because she was with him, and there was a lilt in her voice with a kind of radiance about it when she talked of all she had been doing in his name on the Estate.

She made what she had to relate seem absorbingly interesting, and the Duke was quite surprised to find how long they had been in the Dining-Room.

Only when they went into the Drawing-Room, where the candles were lit and the fragrance of the flowers scented the room, did Alvina say a little hesitatingly:

"There is . . . something . . . I feel I . . . must tell you."

"What is it?" the Duke asked.

"Cousin Jason was here today."

"Jason?"

The name came from the Duke's lips like a pistol-shot.

"Yes, and he was very angry . . . and bitter."

The Duke was silent for a moment. Then he said:

"He must have been on his way to Dover. I told him to leave the country."

"He was very . . . angry!"

"That I can understand. I paid his debts — and they were astronomical — only on condition that he left England, and he will receive the allowance I promised him as long as he stays away."

"I am sure it was very generous of you . . . but he was very upset."

"And he upset you?" the Duke questioned sharply.

"He . . . he . . . cursed you!"

The Duke laughed.

"That does not surprise me. My friend Gerald Chertson said that whatever I did for him, Jason would not be grateful."

There was silence. Then Alvina said:

"He hates you . . . and I am . . . afraid he may . . . hurt you."

The Duke smiled.

"You are not to worry about me. I assure you I can take care of myself."

He saw by the expression on her face that she was really worried, and added:

"I did not survive all those years of fighting against Napoleon's Armies to be exterminated by a rat like Jason!"

"Cornered rats can be . . . dangerous!" Alvina said, speaking as if the words were jerked from her lips.

"Jason is not cornered," the Duke replied. "One of the reasons I was delayed in London was that I was making sure that all his debts were paid in full, and that his allowance would be waiting for him every quarter at a Bank in France. It will, I promise you, be impossible for him to starve."

"I am still frightened for . . . you."

"I refuse to allow Jason to worry either you or me," the Duke replied, "so forget him and let us talk of much more pleasant things."

He saw that Alvina's eyes were still clouded, and said to her quietly:

"I am very grateful to you for worrying about me, but I want you instead to think of yourself."

Alvina raised her eyes to his, and he said:

"We are not going to talk about that tonight, but I will think over what you have said, and I want you to think about it too. We must try to come to some conclusion and agree as to what would be best for you."

"You . . . know the answer to that."

The Duke was about to argue. Then he said:

"Because I did not get to bed until the early hours of the morning, and as I suspect you are too tired after all you have done, I suggest we go to bed. Incidentally, I have not asked you how Miss Richardson is."

"She is not very well," Alvina replied. "She has

been laid up these last two days, but she is being looked after by the new housemaids, and I hope she will be able to get up tomorrow."

"Then I shall look forward to seeing her," the Duke said. "Now I think we should both retire and arrange to meet in the Hall at half-past-seven so that we can have an hour's ride before breakfast."

"That would be wonderful!" Alvina exclaimed. "I was so hoping you would suggest it, and I have been looking forward to seeing you on *Black Knight.*"

The Duke raised his eye-brows.

"Is that the name of my new stallion?"

Alvina looked embarrassed.

"I thought you would not mind my christening him," she said. "He had a horrid name which did not seem appropriate to the Castle."

The Duke laughed.

"Then *Black Knight* he shall be, and one day I will tell you exactly why it is so very appropriate."

"Tell me now."

"Tomorrow," he said. "I need my 'beauty sleep,' and of course you have to live up to your new gowns."

"I have not thanked you properly for them."

"Thank me when the next lot arrives."

He remembered as he spoke that he had asked the Countess of Jersey to choose Alvina's wardrobe for her.

He had ordered two more gowns, which should arrive tomorrow or the next day, but he had thought it would be a mistake for her to have any more before she reached London.

Now he was wondering if all he had planned would have to be changed, and thought that perhaps he had made a mistake in enlisting the help of the Countess of Jersey before he had been certain it was what Alvina wanted.

But he did not wish to discuss it with her at the moment. So he took her by the arm and they walked up the stairs side by side, after the Duke had given orders for the horses to be ready for them in the morning.

When they reached the landing and separated, the Duke to go to his room and Alvina to hers, he said:

"Sleep peacefully, and do not worry. And I promise I will not force you to do anything you really have no wish to do."

She looked up at him as he took her hand in his.

"You are so kind . . . so very . . . very kind, and I . . . want to . . . please you."

"You do please me," he answered, "and if you feel grateful to me, I am grateful to you for all you have done."

"But we have not finished yet," Alvina said quickly.

"We have not finished," the Duke agreed.

"Then . . . good-night, and . . . thank you," she said with a little throb in her voice.

As she spoke she bent her head and kissed his hand.

Then, almost before he realised it had happened, she turned and sped away from him down the passage, disappearing into the darkness as if she were one of the ghosts of the Castle.

The Duke stood still for a second or two after he could see her no more.

Then slowly, as if he was deep in his thoughts, he walked towards his own bedroom.

Alvina, lying in the darkness, found it hard to sleep.

So much had happened during the day, and yet it was as if she had moved in a dream until the Duke had come home.

Then everything had flared into life and become a pulsating, exciting reality so that she felt as if she had suddenly come alive.

"He is back!" she told herself now. "Please, God, let him stay for a very long time."

She had wanted to ask him what he had been doing in London but had felt too shy.

When he said he had been late in getting to bed last night, she supposed he had been enjoying himself with some very beautiful woman who had enthralled and amused him as she was unable to do because she was so ignorant.

She wondered what they had talked about together and if the Duke had paid her compliments. Perhaps when they said "good-night" he had taken her in his arms and kissed her.

Alvina had no idea what a kiss would be like, and yet she thought that if the Duke kissed anybody it would be a very wonderful experience.

'Perhaps it would be like touching the sunlight,' she told herself, 'or feeling a star twinkling against one's breast.'

She had kissed the Duke's hand in gratitude because she had no words in which to tell him how grateful she was for everything he had done since his home-coming.

There was the happiness of the servants as they moved about the great house; the worry which had left the pensioners' eyes; and the satisfaction she had found with the farmers she had visited, once they realised they could repair their buildings and start buying and breeding new stock.

"How can one man, almost as if he were God, change everything overnight?" Alvina asked.

She thought that the Duke exuded a special light which lit up everything and everybody it touched.

"He is wonderful . . . wonderful!" she whispered.

Then, insidiously, as if it were a snake creeping into her thoughts and into the room, she heard Jason's voice cursing him.

She felt herself shiver because of the hatred with which he had spoken and the evil in his eyes which had seemed to vibrate from him.

It had left a darkness on the atmosphere that made her feel she would be afraid to go into the Library again.

"He will hurt the Duke if he can," she told herself, and she knew he wanted him to be dead so that he could be the sixth Duke.

The mere idea of it made her want to cry out in horror.

She was quite certain that there would be no improvements on the Estates if Jason was the Duke, and that in London he would merely dissipate away the money he inherited, or perhaps he would fill the Castle with his dubious friends.

"That must never happen!" she thought, and instinctively she began to pray.

"Take care of the Duke! Please, God, take care of him. Do not let Cousin Jason hurt him, as I know he wishes to."

As she prayed, a sudden idea came into her mind that made her stiffen and lie very still.

When she had found Jason in the house, he was coming from the direction of the Master Suite, and she had wondered why the footmen in the Hall had not told her when she returned from riding that he had called.

It suddenly struck her that they had not done so because they had not known he was in the Castle.

Because he had been there so often when he was a child and later as a young man, he knew the Castle as well as Richard had.

He would be aware that there were dozens of ways leading into it, apart from through the front door.

Now, almost as if somebody were guiding her back into the past, she remembered how Richard and Cousin Ivar had often climbed up the old

Tower in order to show off to each other their skill and nerve.

Because the Tower had been built in mediaeval times, with the stones rough and uncovered with plaster, every one unevenly put in place, it provided easy footholds for anybody experienced at climbing.

She could see, although she must have been very small at the time, her brother and another boy with him holding on to the protruding grey stones and racing each other to the top.

She could hear an echo coming back through the years as Richard cried out:

"I have won!"

Even as she heard his voice echoing back at her, he added:

"You have lost, Jason, and you owe me a bag of sweets!"

'That is how Jason must have got in,' she thought, 'but why? That is the point.'

Even as she asked the question, she knew the answer and in a sudden terror sat up in bed.

Chapter Seven

Moving by instinct because it was dark and there was no time to light a candle, Alvina tore from her bedroom and along the corridor towards the Master Suite on the other side of the Castle.

It was quite a long way, and yet she was driven by an urgency that made her run more quickly than she had ever run before in her life.

Only as she finally reached the outside door did she come to a halt and draw in her breath.

Then she turned the handle and went into the small and elegant Hall off which the Duke's rooms opened.

There was one light flickering low in a sconce on the wall, which guided her to the bedroom door, which she opened without knocking.

As she entered she saw that the Duke had drawn back the curtains and the moonlight was diffusing the room with a magic iridescence which for the moment seemed almost blinding.

Then as she looked towards the bed, the curtains hanging from the heavy canopy made it appear as if there were no-one in it.

The idea that the Duke was already dead made Alvina feel a pain pierce her heart as if it were a dagger.

Strangely, even in that moment of agony, she knew that she loved the Duke.

Then there was a movement from the bed and he exclaimed incredulously:

"Alvina! What is it? What do you want?"

He had gone to bed thinking of her and worrying as to whether he was doing the right thing as far as she was concerned.

Because he was tired, sleep had come to him unexpectedly quickly, and now as he awoke at the opening of the door with the alertness of a man who was used to danger, he was not certain whether he was dreaming it was Alvina or whether she was real.

The moonlight did not reach to where she was standing, and yet he could see somebody white, ethereal, and insubstantial.

The thought passed through his mind that it was a ghost or an apparition such as he had always heard existed in the Castle.

Then he knew it was Alvina and called out her name.

She moved towards the bed.

"It is . . . Jason . . . Cousin Ivar," she said in a breathless tone so that he could barely hear what she said.

The Duke sat up.

"Jason?" he repeated. "What are you talking about?"

"I know how he intends to . . . kill you!"

The Duke stared at Alvina as if he thought he could not be hearing aright what she was saying and must be imagining it.

Now that she was nearer to him, he could see her face quite clearly in the light from the window; her eyes were dark and very large, and he was aware that she was trembling.

"I . . . I did not . . . tell you," she said, "as I . . . should have done . . . but I found him coming from here along the corridor, and he did not enter the Castle by the front door."

"I do not understand."

"You must remember," Alvina went on, "how you and Richard used to climb up the Tower, and both Mama and Papa said that if you did so you were not to climb down again because that was too dangerous, but should come into the house through the trap-door which leads to the staircase inside the tower itself."

Now the Duke understood, and he said:

"Are you suggesting that Jason might enter the Castle in such a strange way to kill me while I am asleep?"

"I am positive that is what he intends to do!" Alvina answered. "Please, Cousin Ivar, believe me, I know that is what he has planned . . . and I can feel the evil of him coming . . . nearer and nearer!"

She wanted to tell the Duke how Jason, after

he had cursed him, had drunk a toast saying: "The Duke is dead! Long live the Duke!" but she thought it would only delay things further.

Instead, she said frantically:

"Get up! Please, get up, and be ready for him! I was only . . . desperately afraid that I was too late to . . . warn you!"

The terror in her voice prevented the Duke from arguing, and he merely said:

"Wait for me outside. I will not be a minute."

Obediently Alvina turned towards the door and went out into the small Hall.

Owing to the draught that she had made when she had opened the door — or perhaps the candle had not been replenished as it should have been — the candle was now extinguished and it was quite dark.

Alvina therefore left the door of the Duke's bedroom ajar, and she could hear him moving about as he dressed himself.

Only as she thought of it was she aware that what she was wearing was very scanty.

She had felt like a Fairy Princess when she went down to dinner in the new gown which the Duke had given her.

So she had, when she went to bed, felt it impossible to put on one of the threadbare and darned nightgowns she had worn for the last few years when her father would not give her any money.

Almost as if it were an auspicious occasion, she had opened the drawer to take out the last nightgown she possessed of those which had belonged to her mother.

It was certainly lovely in contrast to her own, and her mother had worn it seldom because, as she had told Alvina, it was very precious, as her husband had bought it for her on their honeymoon.

Made of soft, almost transparent material, it had frills of shadow lace round the hem, the neck, and the sleeves.

Because her dinner with the Duke had been so enchanting, Alvina had thought that if she looked as attractive in bed as she had at the dining-table, the magic which had encompassed her ever since he had returned would still be with her.

Now, because her nightgown was so transparent, she felt that he might be shocked.

All she had to cover it was a light woollen shawl she had snatched up when she had sprung out of bed.

She had long ago grown out of the dressing-gown she had had when she was a girl, and her father would give her no money with which to buy another.

So the shawl had taken its place, and now a little nervously she made it as long at the back as she could and crossed it over her breasts.

She hoped that the Duke would not notice what she was wearing, but at the same time she felt it was wrong to think of herself when his life was in danger.

She told herself reassuringly that once he had gone up the twisting stone staircase inside the Tower and bolted the trap-door at the top of it, however evil Jason's intentions might be, he would not be able to enter the Castle.

Because Richard and his cousins had insisted upon climbing the Tower, her mother had made the Estate carpenter fix an iron trap into the Tower with bolts on both sides of it.

"I insist on your promising me that when you climb up," she had said firmly, "you will come down through the Tower and back through the house. I know climbing down is far more dangerous than climbing up."

Looking back, Alvina could remember Richard grumbling because he had promised his mother that that was what he would do, and he was too honourable to break his word.

She knew that Jason would pull back the bolts on the trap-door at the top of the Tower, then climb down the twisting stone steps which soldiers had used when the Castle had been built in the Twelfth Century.

She heard the Duke close a drawer and had a sudden fear, as he was taking so long, that long before he could close the trap-door from the inside, Jason would have entered the Castle.

"Hurry!" she cried urgently. "Hurry!"

"I have only been a few minutes," the Duke replied, and opened the door behind her.

He was silhouetted against the moonlight, and she saw that he was wearing a pair of long black pantaloons and a fine linen shirt with a silk scarf round his neck.

She knew, although she could not see his face clearly, that he smiled at her as he said:

"I think, Alvina, this is part of your very fertile imagination, but to make you happy I will close the trap-door at the top of the Tower and bolt it. Then you will be able to sleep peacefully again."

"Thank you," Alvina said, "but . . . please, let us . . . hurry!"

She felt he would not understand if she told him that she could feel the evil that Jason exuded coming nearer and nearer.

The Duke opened the other door and they stepped into the corridor.

There was enough light from just one or two candles that had been left burning for them to see their way to where beyond the Master Suite there was a door that led into the Tower, which was at the extreme end of the building.

As they reached it, Alvina thought that if they found the door was locked, then the Duke would laugh at her for being unnecessarily alarmed.

But it was open, and she was aware that he thought it strange.

Then they were both inside the Tower and standing on the stone steps which led both upwards and downwards, spiralling round a stone pole which had been built in the very centre of the Tower.

There was just enough light from the arrow-slits for them to pick their way without stumbling.

The Duke went first, moving swiftly and almost silently because he was wearing, Alvina realised, bedroom slippers.

It was only as she felt the cold stone under her feet that she realised she was bare-footed.

But nothing mattered except that they should shut Jason out, and as they climbed higher and higher, she did not feel either the cold or the roughness of the stones which bruised the softness of her skin.

They reached the top, and, finding the trapdoor shut, the Duke turned his head to say:

"Your fears, Alvina, were unnecessary."

As he spoke he reached up his hand and found that the inside bolts were pulled back and it was not locked as it should have been.

Then, as he pushed, the trap-door swung open and the moonlight flooded in.

"It was not bolted!" Alvina said almost beneath her breath.

Then, to her consternation, instead of bolting it on the inside as she wanted him to do, the Duke stepped out onto the roof, and turning put his hand out to pull her out too.

They now stood on the sloping leads.

These had been added very much later to prevent the water from accumulating on the top of the Tower and percolating down the sides of the new part of the house.

It was easy to stand without slipping because

her feet were bare, and the Duke, having drawn her beside him, said:

"It is years since I have been up here, and I had forgotten how high it is, but of course in the daytime there is the finest view over the country-side one could possibly imagine."

As he spoke he moved away from her towards the side of the Tower to look out over the valley which lay to the right of the Castle, and which, bathed in moonlight, was very beautiful.

Even as he did so, Alvina heard a sound on the other side of the Tower and saw a man's head appear.

She made an inarticulate little sound of fear.

But before the Duke could turn round, Jason had swung himself over the parapet and was standing on the Tower, balancing himself, as the Duke had been forced to do, on the sloping leads.

"Quite a reception-party, I see!" he said sarcastically. "I suppose our interfering, tiresome little Cousin Alvina thought I might be visiting you to-night?"

"What are you doing here, Jason?" the Duke asked sharply. "You should be in Dover by now."

"I will reach Dover tomorrow morning," Jason replied, "where I shall be told that, most regrettably, my dear cousin the Duke of Harlington has met with an unfortunate accident during the night."

As he spoke he drew from his waist a long, thin, evil-looking knife of the sort Alvina imagined a brigand or a pirate might use, but which she had not seen before except in pictures.

She gave a cry of horror and realised, even as she did so, that when Jason had said that the Duke would die painfully, this was what he was planning.

Too late, she thought wildly that she should have made the Duke bring some weapon with him.

But she had never envisaged for one moment that he would come out onto the roof, but rather that he would bolt the trap-door to make it impossible for Jason to enter the Castle.

The Duke, however, was looking at his cousin with contempt.

"Do you really imagine that you can murder me and not be hanged for your crime?"

"It is unfortunate that you were foolish enough to come up to the Tower when you could have died far more comfortably in your bed," Jason sneered, "and to bring that tiresome chit Alvina with you was an even greater mistake."

"Certainly from your point of view," the Duke said. "Criminals always dislike a witness to their crime."

He was talking normally, but at the same time he was trying to work out how he could reach Jason and knock him out without being badly wounded by the long blade of the knife which was now pointing towards him.

The Duke never under-estimated an enemy, and he knew he had been stupid and foolhardy to have come up on the Tower empty-handed while Jason was sure to be well armed.

The Duke knew it was the sort of knife that could pierce deeply into a man's body, and if it entered his heart there would be no chance of anybody being able to save his life.

"Alvina will of course have an unfortunate fall from the top of the Tower," Jason replied in answer to the Duke's last remark, "while you will have impaled yourself, quite by accident, of course, on the knife, which will have only your finger-prints on it."

"Very carefully planned!" the Duke exclaimed. "At the same time, Jason, things seldom work out exactly as one wishes them to do, and I warn you that I shall fight ferociously both to live and to ensure that you do not take my place as the next Duke."

Jason's laugh sounded eerie and not human.

Now he moved a little farther up the sloping roof so as to be higher than the Duke, and he was pointing the knife at him almost as if it were a sword.

Alvina knew that in such a position it was almost impossible for the Duke to approach him without being wounded or perhaps killed in the attempt.

It was easy to see that Jason, without his fancy coat and wearing only a shirt, was far stronger and more athletic than he appeared when dolled up as a Dandy.

Alvina could see the muscles in his arms and

knew, as she had told the Duke, that like a cornered rat he would fight dangerously, unsportingly, unfairly, because from his point of view there was so much at stake.

She had become so frightened while the two men were talking that she felt as if her legs would no longer support her.

Now she sank down on the leads, half-kneeling, half-sitting, feeling her heart beat tumultuously in her breast from sheer terror.

As she watched the two men eying each other, Jason waiting to strike to kill, she felt desperately that only God could save the Duke.

"Save him! Save him!" she prayed frantically. "Oh, God, let him live!"

She felt as if every instinct, every nerve in her body, was tense with the agonising plea of her prayer.

Then, because she felt almost as if she would faint at the horror of what was happening, she put out her hand to steady herself, and felt something hard lying on the leads beside her.

She thought it was a stone.

Then as her fingers closed over it, she realised it was a hand that must have become detached from one of the statues which decorated the roof of the centre block to which the Tower was attached.

Without thinking, she held on to it tightly, and as she did so, an idea came to her.

It was almost as if Richard were beside her, saying as he had in the old days:

"Come on, 'Vina, try to bowl like a man rather than throw like a woman!"

So she had learnt to do what he told her, and when there was nobody better to play with him, she had bowled to him so that he could practise his batting for the Cricket XI at Eton.

The two men were still watching each other closely, and because she loved him Alvina knew that the Duke was thinking his only chance was to spring at Jason and topple him over before he had a chance to drive the knife into his body.

It was a slender chance, a very slender one, because Jason was on a higher level than he was, and his hatred had given him in some ways a superior strength.

The Duke made one last plea.

"Put down that deadly weapon, Jason," he said, "and let us talk this over sensibly. I will even arrange that you shall have more money than I have already promised when you reach France."

"I do not want your money," Jason snarled, "I want your title, and that is what I intend to have! Then I shall be head of the family — I, Jason Harling, whom you have all despised — and you will be dead, damn you!"

As he spoke he made a stabbing gesture with the knife, and Alvina had a sudden fear that he might throw it at the Duke.

Raising her arm, she threw the stone hand with all her strength in exactly the way Richard had taught her, aiming at Jason's head.

It flew through the air, catching him on the

side of his cheek below the eye with a violence that threw him off balance.

He staggered, but he was standing precariously on the sloping roof, and his feet slipped.

He tried to save himself, dropping the knife as he flung out his hands towards the higher level of the castellated parapet, but he missed and staggered again.

Then, so swiftly that it was hard to believe it was happening, he tripped over the lower part of the wall, and there was just one last glimpse of his feet silhouetted against the sky before he disappeared completely.

As he did so, Alvina gave a muffled cry and, rising, flung herself against the Duke to hide her face on his shoulder.

She was trembling so violently that he put his arms round her, for the shock and terror of what had happened had made her unable to stand alone.

Then, as he heard her gasping for breath as if she had been near drowning, he said very quietly:

"It is all right, my darling, you saved my life, and he will not trouble either of us any more!"

As Alvina felt she could not have heard him aright, she raised her face to look up at him in bewilderment.

Then as he looked down at her in the moonlight, he pulled her closer still and his lips came down on hers.

Only as he kissed her did Alvina know that this was what she had been longing for, wanting, and dreaming about, but she had never thought it would happen.

For a moment the closeness of him, the comfort of his arms, and the fact that he was alive were all a part of his lips.

Then as his kiss became more insistent, more possessive, she felt her fear vanish, and instead there was a wonder like a shaft of golden sunshine moving up from her breast into her throat.

It was so wonderful, so perfect, so much a part of her dreams and the moonlight, that she felt it was she who must have died and reached a Heaven in which there was no fear but only the Duke and the wonder of him.

When he kissed her, the Duke knew to his astonishment that he had found, when he had least expected it, what he had been searching for all his life.

As he felt the softness of Alvina's lips beneath his, he knew that she was not only part of the Castle and the ideals he had had of it when he was young, but the love he had thought was unobtainable because it only existed in fairy-stories and his dreams.

The feelings she was arousing in him were fine and spiritual, and different in every way from what he had felt for any other woman.

They were also part of the honour and chivalry that had always lain at the back of his mind, being the ideal for which all men should strive.

He knew as he held Alvina closer and still closer to him that this was what he had wanted to find in the woman he made his wife but had thought it impossible.

Only when he was aware that she was quivering in his arms, but very differently from when she had turned to him in fear and horror, did he raise his head to say:

"My precious — I love you!"

"You . . . love me?" she whispered. "And I . . . love you. I knew tonight when I thought you might . . . die that if you did . . . I must die too."

Because what she felt had been so intense, so terrifying, for a moment the fear was back in her eyes and in her voice.

Then, as if it was unimportant, she asked:

"Did you . . . really say that you . . . loved me?"

"I love you," the Duke confirmed, "and, my darling, what could be more appropriate than you should have saved my life, so that now I can dedicate it to you, and to everything you wish me to do for all time."

Alvina gave a little cry, and lifting her face to his she said:

"You are so . . . wonderful! I knew God could not let you die . . . and when I prayed . . . He told me what to do!"

As if her words made the Duke remember what they had passed through and that they were still standing on top of the Tower, with Jason dead on the ground below, he said:

"Let us get away from here. It will be easier to talk inside."

Alvina did not move. Instead she said:

"I shall . . . always remember that it was here . . . with your head against the stars . . . that you . . . first kissed me."

Because the way she spoke sounded as if she was enchanted, the Duke kissed her again, his lips holding her captive, his arms making it hard for her to breathe.

Yet she felt as if they were both enveloped by something sacred, something very spiritual and part of God.

Then, as if he forced himself to be sensible, the Duke said:

"Go down the stairs, my darling. I wish to be rid of that unpleasant weapon before I join you."

As she drew away from him, Alvina realised that when she had run to him after Jason's fall, she had left her shawl behind.

Now she put her hands up to her breasts, blushed, and said:

"I am sorry . . . I forgot I was only . . . wearing a nightgown."

The Duke smiled.

"You look very lovely, my darling, if a little un-conventional."

Then, as if she excited him, he pulled her back into his arms and kissed her again.

His kiss was different from what it had been before, more demanding, more passionate, but at the same time he kept control of his desire, fearing to frighten her.

As he felt her surrender herself to his insis-tence, he knew that while the softness and warmth of her excited him, so that his body throbbed for her, it was still something very different from anything he had felt before.

Perhaps reverence was the right word, or simply love, the real love he never expected to find.

He raised his head to look down at Alvina's radiant face and shining eyes.

"I love you," he said as if it was a vow.

"I love you until there is nothing . . . else . . . in the whole world but you," she whispered.

Then as the Duke let her go, she blushed again and bent to pick up her shawl, before she moved carefully towards the trap-door.

As she did so, the Duke climbed over the sloping roof to where on the other side of it Jason had dropped the long, sharp knife with which he had intended to kill him.

He picked it up, and then, feeling as if it was an omen of the future, he flung the knife, gleaming evilly in the moonlight, over the side of the Tower.

He knew it would fall into a clump of thick shrubs, where it would doubtless be a very long time before it was discovered.

As he did so, he felt that he threw from himself and Alvina everything that was wicked and dangerous, and that now he could protect and keep her, and all those who depended on him, safe for as long as he should live.

Then as he turned towards the trap-door, he took one quick glance over the side of the Tower.

Vaguely in the shadow of the Tower he could see, spread-eagled on the ground far below, the prostrate form of Jason Harling.

The Duke knew there was no chance that after falling from such a great height he could still be alive, and in the morning when he was found he would think up an explanation.

He could say that Jason had wished to climb the Tower for the last time before he left England, and nobody need ever know there was any other reason for such an exploit.

Turning away, the Duke followed Alvina, who was moving down the twisting staircase towards the door which led to the end of the corridor.

He pulled the trap-door to behind him, but he did not bolt it.

He felt as he left it open that it was symbolic of the fact that there was no longer anything to fear, and that not only his life but the contents of the Castle and the people who lived there were also safe.

They were under the protection of the Power that had saved him from what he was well aware might have been an ignominious death.

He reached the door into the corridor and Alvina was waiting. He thought as she looked up at him that an inner light illuminated her face.

He put his arms round her as together they walked towards the Master Suite and in through the door they had left open.

The bedroom was still bathed in moonlight, and the Duke took Alvina to the open window.

They looked out over the lake, which was a pool of silver, and at the great trees in the Park, their leaves shining above their dark trunks.

With a little sigh Alvina spoke for the first time.

"Now we need no . . . longer be . . . afraid."

"That is true," the Duke said. "I will protect and look after you, and as my wife there will be for you no fears, only happiness."

Alvina gave a little cry that was almost child-like and said:

"Is it . . . true . . . really true that you . . . love me?"

"It will take me a long time to tell you how much," the Duke replied. "I know now that you are the ideal person I dream of, and who was always in a secret shrine in my heart."

He pulled her closer before he went on:

"I have travelled a long way to find you, my precious one, and now that I have done so, I will never let you go! You are mine!"

She turned her face up to his, and she thought he would kiss her, but instead he said:

"You will not go to London, you will not be acclaimed as a Society Beauty. You will stay here with me, and I warn you I shall be very jealous if you want anything else."

Alvina laughed, and it was like the song of the birds in spring.

"Oh, darling, wonderful Ivar! You know I want nothing more than to be here in the Castle with . . . you, but I still cannot believe that you . . . love me."

"I will make you sure of it."

"But I do not know how to . . . amuse you like the beautiful women you know in Paris and in London, and perhaps after a little while you will find me very boring."

The Duke smiled, and he knew as he thought back of the women in his life, that like Isobel they had always ultimately bored him.

The reason why he always wished to escape from them was that they could not give him what Alvina could.

"Someday," he said very quietly, "I will make you understand that the love we have for each other is very different from anything I have ever found or known before."

"Is that true?"

"I promise you it is true," he said, "and just as when I was a boy, the Castle stood for me for everything that was fine and noble, so I have always thought in my heart that the woman who reigned here with me must be fine, noble, beautiful, and also must love me, but *nobody else*."

He accentuated the last words, thinking of how he had always loathed the idea of being married to somebody who would deceive him with other lovers.

He had also disliked the knowledge that he was not the first man in their lives, but was probably following a succession of other men who had possessed them.

Because Alvina was so different, he felt frightened that she might change, and pulling her almost roughly against him he added:

"You are mine, mine completely, and if you stop loving me I think I would strangle you, or throw you from the Tower as Jason intended to do!"

He was speaking in a way so unlike his usual iron control that it flashed through his mind that he had frightened her.

Instead, she gave a little laugh and pressed herself closer to him.

"How can you imagine I could ever look at anybody else besides you?" she asked. "I have not known many men, but I know that nobody could be kinder, or more like the Knights who used to live here in the Castle."

Because she was thinking as he had, the Duke looked at her in surprise as she went on:

"I sometimes think those Knights are still here with us, and when I have been lonely and afraid because Papa was very angry with me, they seemed to be guarding me and telling me that one day things would be different."

She gave a deep sigh that seemed to come from the very depths of her being as she added:

"Then you came, and you were a Knight in Shining Armour, to kill the Dragon that was destroying everything."

"I think you did that," the Duke said quietly, "and it is something, my precious, that you must never tell anybody, or even think about again."

"I do not think it was . . . wrong of me to . . . kill Cousin Jason," Alvina said, "because I knew that if he killed you, so many people would suffer . . . perhaps in an even worse way than they did with Papa."

"We will never talk about it again," the Duke said firmly. "Instead, I want only to think of you and to kiss you."

His lips came down on hers, and he kissed her until she felt that the moonlight was not only round them but on their lips, in their hearts, and in their very souls.

She knew that the Duke was right when he had said that together they would make the Castle a place of nobility and honour for all those who looked to them for guidance.

Perhaps too it would shine like a beacon of light to help those in other parts of the country who were in desperate need of help.

Alvina felt that the generations of people who had lived in the Castle before them were supporting them and giving them strength in the great task which lay ahead.

Because she had saved the Duke's life, she no longer felt insignificant or unsure of herself as she had done in the past.

She knew he would always be her master, her guide, and her protector, but she knew too that she had something to give him, and that was love, real love, which he said he had not found in his life until now.

She reached up her arms towards him and did

not notice that her shawl fell to the floor.

"I love you . . . I love you! Teach me to do . . . exactly as you want me to do, and I know, because God has blessed us . . . that I shall be able to make you . . . happy."

"I am happy, my lovely one!" the Duke answered. "Happier than I have ever been before and we will express our gratitude by making everybody round us happy too."

He kissed her forehead, her straight little nose, her chin, and then the softness of her neck.

He felt her quiver with an excitement she had never known before, and knew she excited him to madness.

"God, how I love you," he said.

His voice was deep and unsteady as he added:

"How soon will you marry me? I cannot wait to make you my wife!"

"I am ready now . . . at this moment . . . or tomorrow!" Alvina replied impulsively.

He laughed tenderly before he said:

"That is what I wanted you to say, and I will arrange it."

"Can we be married here . . . in the Chapel?"

He knew she looked at him a little anxiously in case he should want something different, and he replied:

"Of course! I can think of nothing more appropriate than that we should be married, not with a large number of friends and acquaintances to watch us, but with those who have lived and died in the Castle and are still here, watching over us."

Because it was just what she thought herself, Alvina made a murmur of joy.

Then she asked:

"How can you think . . . exactly as I do? How can you believe as I . . . believe? And how can you . . . want what I want?"

"The answer to that is quite simple," the Duke replied. "We are one person, my precious one, and when you are my wife you will find that our life together will be very full, very exciting, and indeed very satisfying, because together we are complete."

Alvina gave a cry of sheer happiness.

Then he was kissing her again, kissing her passionately, demandingly, possessively, and she could feel his heart beating frantically against hers.

She knew as the moonlight within them seemed to intensify until it filled the whole world that there was nothing else but their love.

They had passed through great dangers to find each other, and neither of them would ever be alone again.

We hope you have enjoyed this Large Print book. Other G.K. Hall & Co. or Chivers Press Large Print books are available at your library or directly from the publishers.

For more information about current and upcoming titles, please call or write, without obligation, to:

G.K. Hall & Co.
295 Kennedy Memorial Drive
Waterville, ME 04901 USA
Tel. (800) 223-1244
      (800) 223-6121

OR

Chivers Press Limited
Windsor Bridge Road
Bath BA2 3AX
England
Tel. (0225) 335336

All our Large Print titles are designed for easy reading, and all our books are made to last.